Sherlock Holmes
THE SHRIEKING PITS

Nikki Nelson-Hicks

Third Crow Press

ISBN: 978-1-7320967-8-3

Third Crow Press
640 Bradford Drive
Gallatin, TN USA 37066

Sherlock Holmes; The Shrieking Pits, Nikki Nelson-Hicks. – 2nd Edition
Previously Published by Pro Se Press but without the cool pics.
Illustrations from The Strand, 1893-1902, Sidney Paget
Book Layout © 2016 BookDesignTemplates.com
Third Crow Logo by Brenna Gael Designs
Dave Brzeski, Editor
Cover art and logo by Jeffrey Haynes,
Plasmafire Graphics, jeffreyrayhayes@gmail.com

For Brian Hicks, my own Watson.

CONTENTS

CHAPTER ONE

THE EXPERIMENT

The last time I saw Sherlock Holmes was towards the end of a harsh, bleak winter. It was so cold that blocks of ice floated down the Thames and the papers reported birds had frozen solid on the shoulders of Lord Nelson's statue in Trafalgar Square.

Alas, the mood in 221B Baker Street was no warmer.

I found the door locked so I knocked upon the thin wooden frame. "Holmes? Hello, It's Watson. Are you accepting visitors today?"

"Watson? Of course! Come in, come in. Use the key secreted above the door frame."

My fingers nimbly pushed aside the false panel above the doorframe and retrieved the key. I opened the door to find my friend on the floor, in front of the fireplace, cross-legged and sitting so close I feared the fire would ignite his dressing gown. He was tearing out strips from pages of the Strand, crumbling them into balls, and tossing them into the flame.

I took off my coat, set down my bags, pushed some papers and books out of my favorite chair and sat down. "Holmes, I am afraid to ask but, what, pray tell, are you doing?"

"It's an experiment. I am attempting to deduce what sort of chemical agents are used in the ink by the printers of this abominable rag by gauging the changing color in the flame."

"Chemical agents? Like a poison? Are you suggesting that the publishers of the Strand are poisoning their readers?"

"With some sort of neurological agent, something that shrinks the mind and twists the brain."

"And you had to use an edition with one of my pieces in it?"

Holmes tossed the rest of the paper into the fire, stood up as gracefully as a cat and closed the cast iron screen as the flames crackled and popped. "It doesn't matter. The experiment was a failure. No conclusive evidence."

"And which one of my stories has fired up your contempt this time? Let me guess. Was it the one about the Scarlet Tapestry or the Sugar Glass Killer?"

"There must be something in the ink!" He stood and faced me in a flash. "It's the only logical conclusion as to why people would continue to dabble in this twaddle!" he said and then threw himself into his chair.

"Holmes..."

"So, how long will you be gone? I hope you remembered to get the right gauge of fishing line this time."

"How...?" I stopped myself from engaging him in this game. I knew how he delighted in observing me attempt to fathom the brambles of his mind, but I was in no mood to finance his whimsies. "I will be gone for three or four months. There is a medical symposium in Switzerland I have been invited to speak at, following which I have been invited to a friend's hunting lodge for some fishing, and then..."

"... and then you'll be doubtless retreating to some godforsaken cabin to compose more lurid tales for your taskmaster at the Strand. I gathered as much from the shopping bag at your feet. Full of notebooks—the horrible lined sort that smell like glue and mold—the sort you prefer to use when you are woolgathering. So, just go and scribble away more of your lurid tales, turning me, more and more, into a caricature, a figment of fiction. Still, this could be a godsend. Perhaps, in your absence, I will have the congenial silence of solitude that I am so deprived of when you are underfoot!"

I pushed myself angrily out of my chair, walked to the window, took a deep breath and slowly released it. I knew he was baiting me, trying to get me to stay and endure with him the long London winter and I didn't want to leave on bad terms. My friend was a challenging companion at the best of times but during his dark moods, like the ones that the gray clouds of the season often inspired in him, he could be insufferable.

"I will keep in touch as much, as I can," I said, keeping my voice light. "telegrams and the like, in case you do need me."

"Don't worry about me, my dear fellow. I'll be fine. I have a dozen cases just waiting for me." He nodded towards a pile of letters that were pinned to the mantle by a Bowie knife.

"Oh? You do? How wonderful. May I see?"

"Please do." He stretched out his long legs until I feared his feet would burn on the grate. "I suspect they are just the sort of thing you would appreciate."

I plucked the knife from out of the stack. The return address on the first envelope was The London Society of Psychical Research. I flipped through the rest, over a dozen in all, and saw the same on each.

"Was I not correct, Watson? Surely there is some fodder in that batch to satisfy your readers?"

"Holmes..."

He jumped up from the couch with more energy he'd displayed in days and snatched the letters from my hand. "Oh, do let me recite one or two. I have them scorched into my mind. This one is regarding a haunted castle with a banshee. These half a dozen are regarding fairy abductions. Fairies! And this one, oh dear boy, this one is my personal favorite: a talking mongoose!" Holmes tossed them up in the air and they cascaded around him as he threw himself back into his chair. "A mongoose, Watson! Talking or otherwise, it is all a bore to me."

I sat across from my friend. The deep blue satin of his dressing gown made his pale skin all that more translucent. His arms hung over the armchair and his long, slender fingers fidgeted as if burning with electricity. His hair was unkempt and hung over his forehead and into his eyes, shading his intense gray stare that gazed into the fire as if to challenge it to a duel. The chaos of the room around me also spoke volumes. A tray with untouched plates of food sat cold on the buffet. A dozen cups, some empty and some only half filled, perched on mantle spaces and on top of towers of books. Empty beakers and cold Bunsen burners sat unused on the kitchen table. The cold winter outside had frozen not only the Thames but whatever fire kept Holmes' mind alight and I feared for my friend's health.

"That's it, then," I said and clapped my hands as a gesture of finality. "There's nothing more to be done. I am not going, Holmes. Not with you in this state."

His eyes flickered over to me and he shook his head. "No. Don't be absurd, Watson. These moods of mine never last. You of all people should know that by now." He stood, picked up my bag and coat and led me towards the door. "You worry too much. Like a fat, mother hen. Something will come up. Besides, I have other means of distraction."

I stopped him at the door. "It is those means that worry me. I am your doctor as well as your friend. I can see that you are in a very bad way indeed, and I know where that way leads. Someone needs to be here with you."

Holmes sighed deeply and waved me away with his long, pallid hand. "Time away from me is probably best for both of us. Come back when London is awake and living again."

CHAPTER TWO

MISSING!

"HOLDING IT ONLY AN INCH OR TWO FROM HIS EYES."

Those words haunted me all those months abroad. I kept in touch with telegrams and he, in turn, kindly responded once or twice but, since the end of April, I had heard no word from my friend. I thought to contact others but, knowing of Sherlock Holmes' preternatural need for privacy, I abstained. I was happy when my fishing trip was cut short as I was desperate to check on the well-being of my friend as soon as I returned home to London.   You can imagine my irritation as Violet, my housekeeper, informed me that I had guests.

"They are waiting for you in your office, sir. A gentleman and his companion... a lady... one of those Oriental ladies, if you know what I mean, sir," she said with an arched brow. "Not that I make judgments, sir."

I sighed. "Who are they?"

She gave me a calling card that read in bold, golden print: **Mr. Ulysses K. Todd, London Society of Psychical Research**.

"Who the blazes is this?" I said, irked at the imposition. "Why does he want to see me?"

"He was adamant on giving you his condolences in person, sir."

"Condolences? For what?"

"Why, for Mr. Holmes, sir," she said as she took my coat and hat. "Mr. Todd said he had Mr. Holmes' personal effects, that he'd like to return."

"What!" I cried out in shock. "What has happened to Holmes?"

"I thought you knew, sir." She handed over the evening paper that she had folded under her arm. "It's been in all the papers, sir."

I shook my head. I had not read a paper in ages as it was my custom, when I go on writing sabbatical, to completely cut myself off from everything except the adventure I was attempting to bring to life. My hands shook as I unfolded the paper and there on the front page was a very flattering illustration of Holmes and the headline: SHERLOCK HOLMES: MISSING!!!

"Oh my God... Holmes!" All the premonitions and ill forebodings I had flooded over me. I felt the blood rush from my face, and I feared for a second that I might faint.

As luck would have it, Violet, that dear old girl who had been so good to my late wife, Mary, in her final days, came to my rescue. She led me to a chair, looked deeply into my eyes, and laid a heavy hand on my shoulder.

"Don't you worry, sir. It's not as if this is the first time for Mr. Holmes to go missing. I'll bring you in a hot pot of tea to your office. Mr. Todd and his, erm, lady friend, are just inside. I'm sure you'll get this sorted out in no time."

I watched her walk towards the mysterious domain of Violet's Kitchen. The only person she ever allowed to cross that border was Mary and that was only after three years of marriage to me. It was as if Violet was testing her, to see if she was going to stay long enough to get attached to her. After Mary died, Violet Cabot once again closed the kitchen off to everyone. I sometimes think Violet took Mary's death as an insult to her loyalty.

I looked at the headline again. SHERLOCK HOLMES: MISSING!!! Holmes' ascetic face looked back at me from above the fold, as if mocking such an overuse of exclamation points.

I skimmed the article, my eyes hooked on only the important facts: Sherlock Holmes, reported missing in Almertune- in the county of Norfolk, three days ago, near a local landmark called the Shrieking Pits, in the company of a team investigating the existence of fairies, Scotland Yard has yet to release a statement—

Wait. Fairies? I read the word again. FAIRIES? Sherlock Holmes, champion of hard logic and deductive reasoning? Sherlock Holmes, who had delighted in ribbing me for being a romantic and peddler of lurid tales? Sherlock Holmes had gone missing looking for fairies? In Norfolk, of all places? NORFOLK? There is nothing in Norfolk but beach and peat. What in God's name was he doing out there? And what deviltry befell him?

I thumbed the calling card. London Society of Psychical Research. It rang a bell. Where had I seen that before? I cast around inside my brain trying to remember. I could almost remember but then it would slide away. So many months had passed since I saw Holmes, everything was a jumbled mess. I would need to calm my fears and become a thinking machine, like my friend, if I wanted to be of any service to him.

I could almost hear Holmes taunting me: *You know my methods, Watson, use them! Find me! Think, Watson! Think!*

"Right." I folded the paper and tucked it under my arm. "Let the game begin."

CHAPTER THREE

WHAT BETTER PRIZE?

I entered my office nervously, pretending Sherlock Holmes was at my side to guide me. It was a mere trick of psychology, I know, an imaginary comfort, but it calmed me nevertheless. It was his incredible gifts of deduction that had saved the day so many times. I was merely a scribe, scribbling down words, doing my best to keep up and share with the world the wonder of the incredible insight and powers of deduction that my friend infuriatingly took as elementary.

Frankly, even after all the years I had spent under his tutelage, I still felt like an awkward schoolboy being called up to the blackboard to solve some impossible mathematic equation. With a broken stick. In Latin.

Go on, old boy, pray tell, what do you observe?

My office served as a consulting room; the first-place patients would see as they came for an examination. It's a comfortable sized room and one of my favorites. Mary thought that it should be a welcoming place and so decorated it like a parlor. She chose light tan wallpaper with deep burgundy Persian blossoms that looked like rolling waves scrolling across the wall. To the west, walnut bookcases lined the walls. They not only held medical journals but also decorative knick-knacks. A phrenology skull teetered on the top shelf. Mary thought it was morbid, but it was a birthday gift from Holmes and the one piece that I insisted stay. To the east, there was my desk with two chairs for patients. The window behind my desk provided sunshine for a jungle of ferns and greenery that Mary stacked in vases and planters. She firmly believed that the plants produced excess oxygen that promoted health and vitality. As far as I was concerned, the mess of foliage merely attracted bugs and dust. To the north, there was the door that led to my examination room. To the South, was the fireplace, unlit and, in front of it, there stood a man.

Good. Excellent description of what you already knew. I could see Holmes rolling his eyes at my incompetence. *Now, list your impressions of the man.*

His name is Ulysses K. Todd, if the card is to be believed. Young, late twenties. Dark hair. Light blue eyes. Well groomed. From his suit and shoes, he is wealthy, but I do not believe he earned his fortune through work. His hands, too soft. But he's athletic, well-muscled. Wrestling? Something that works his whole body. Gentry, then. Old money. He's taller than he appears because he stoops a little, 6' 1" maybe, full height, lists to the side when he stands, scoliosis?... ah, his shoe!

Good... well done.

His right shoe was thick, clumsy. An orthopedic! This man has a club foot! That explains why he leans, to alleviate the discomfort of the shoe. That explained why he stood even though it is obviously a great burden to him.

Now, observe closer. What sort of man is he?

Nervous. His nails are bitten down to the quick. He was a very anxious man, simply buzzing with tremendous nervous energy. He had nearly worn a groove in my rug from where he had paced back and forth. There was a desperate air about him, something fragile, crystalline even, as if the weight of the world would break him if—

Tut, tut. No need to wax lyrical. Stick to what we can actually observe. Now, what of the woman?

She was sitting in the chair in front of my desk. Well-groomed in a fashionable lilac walking dress. Early thirties, I'd say. Medium build. Athletic. She had strong, veiny hands, like those of a potter. She had definite Japanese features, olive skin, beautiful hazel eyes and chestnut hair kept in a loose bun under her hat. She kept her eyes steadily on Mr. Todd, watching him with an analytical, almost medical, gaze. She sat as if perched but ready to jump at a moment's notice. A matronly air, as if she—

Watson...

At her feet, there are two bags. One is a green and blue carpetbag. It is well used, threadbare in places. She keeps it close to her for safety as well as for easy access as women often do so I suspect that it belongs to her. The other is a piece of luggage, a leather valise with brass handles, which I recognize as belonging to Sherlock Holmes.

Interesting...now off you go! The game is afoot!

"Oh, Doctor Watson!" Upon noticing me at the door, the young man, Mr. Todd, rushed towards me, his hands in supplication. The strength of his hands gave credence to my theory of his time in the wrestling ring. A strange herbal odor wafted off him. I made a mental note and added that nugget to my profile.

"Doctor Watson! Oh, sir! Please, please accept my apologies. I had no idea, none whatsoever that Mr. Holmes would be in danger when I asked him to accompany me on my investigation of the Bloody Woman of the Shrieking Pit."

The woman rushed up behind him. She was surprisingly tall, 5' 9" or so. "Ulysses, please. Give him room to breathe." She clasped her hand around his arm and held him back. She smiled at me with closed lips and nodded. "Excuse him, Dr. Watson, the wait has only wound up his already strained nerves."

I fought the instinct to apologize for the wait as is my own custom, which Holmes has often chided me on. If I were going to go about this in the same vein as Holmes, I had to act the part. "I understand. Please, have a seat."

They settled in the client chairs and I sat across from them. I leaned back and templed my fingers under my chin as I had seen Holmes do countless times. The sight of him closing his eyes and resting his chin on his slender fingers always invoked a sense of confidence and mystique. I fear my stumpy hands looked clumsier than monastic, but I endured.

"First, introductions," I said. "I assume you are Mr. Ulysses K. Todd of the London Society of Psychical Research? Yes? And, pray tell, who is your companion?"

"Permit me to introduce Mrs. Bernadette Dowell, my nurse and personal secretary."

"Ah, a secretary. She accompanies you on your investigations, does she? How... unconventional."

I could see Mrs. Dowell's cheeks flush. She leaned forward to speak but Mr. Todd put his hand gently on her arm and glanced at her, his brows tense. She acquiesced and sat back.

"Dr. Watson, I feel completely at fault for whatever has befallen Mr. Holmes. If he hadn't caved into my repeated requests for his help in my unconventional investigations, he would be safe and sound here in London."

"And what do you think happened to Sherlock Holmes?"

"Obviously, he was taken to serve in the court of Lord Oberon, King of the Fairies, of course."

I fear my jaw dropped as my hands fell from beneath my chin and dropped to my lap.

"I see," I said, although I obviously didn't. I stared into his pale blue eyes and saw absolute trust and genuine sympathy. Mrs. Dowell looked away when I turned towards her; she shifted in her seat and bit her lip.

"Yes." I opened my desk drawer and pulled out a blank notepad and a freshly sharpened pencil. God bless Violet. She kept my desk stocked the way Mary always did, rest her soul. I instantly felt better with the wooden pencil in my hand and a fresh pad of paper. That, at least, gave me some comfort, some sense of normalcy and propriety. "Let's start at the beginning, shall we? When did you first contact Sherlock Holmes?"

"I had been sending him letters for months now. I was confident that if I could involve someone like Sherlock Holmes, with his reputation for scientific inquiry and impeachable record, it would lend more credence to my bid for admittance into the Society."

"But you list the London Society of Psychical Research on your calling card. A bit presumptuous, wouldn't you say?"

Mrs. Dowell grinned at that remark.

"Simply thinking ahead, Doctor Watson." Mr. Todd tapped his heavily shod foot on the floor in a nervous rat-a-tat-tat. Mrs. Dowell put a calming hand on his shoulder and the tapping ceased immediately. "It is merely a matter of time before my research is given the gravitas that it deserves. And once my theories are verified, I will be begged to join the Society. That is a certainty."

I looked to Mrs. Dowell but her face was stoic, purposefully so.

"Of course, I am sorry for any misunderstanding. Please, continue with your account."

Mr. Todd took a deep breath in an effort to steady his nerves, but it was a wasted motion. He still vibrated with tension as he started to tell his tale.

"As I said, I had been, as Mrs. Dowell so often called it, 'pestering' Mr. Holmes for his help on many of my past investigations but he never responded. No matter how vehemently, I begged, he simply ignored me. It was vexing! I offered to pay his full passage if he came with me to America to search for Sasquatch, but I heard nothing. Then there was the trip to Mongolia to seek out the Death Worm and still, he was silent. Haunted castles, talking animal spirits pestering farmhouses. Nothing seemed to inspire his imagination! I had nearly given up hope until a few weeks ago, in late April, when I received a letter from Mr. Holmes accepting the offer to accompany me on my investigation of the Bloody Woman of the Shrieking Pits."

I stopped my scribbling. "Wait. What Bloody Woman of the Shrieking Pits? The papers said that Holmes disappeared while hunting fairies."

"Ah, the press. The bane of my existence." Mr. Todd's hand went nervously to his mouth; Mrs. Dowell gently patted his knee, reminding him of his habit and he made a fist and put it back down in his lap. "Yes, well, the newspapers, looking for a quick headline, got it wrong—as usual. I wasn't there hunting for fairies, per se. I was looking for a portal, a doorway between this plane and the realm of the Fae."

"I see. And the Shrieking Pits? This is where—?"

Todd's eyes glistened brightly; his voice was rapid and breathless as if he needed to be reminded to take a breath. "Ah, that is where it gets clever. You see, the legends surrounding the pits—they are these strange circular indentations in the ground, some as large as a house, some as small as a well—the legends are contaminated with the idea that these circles are actually the remains of ancient pagan dwellings and the screams. Supposedly, there are horrible shrieking screams that come from these circles at certain times of the year—not surprisingly during the Solstices, when the veil between this world and others is stretched thin. The legends say that these screams are the death wails of sacrificial victims as they are murdered by pagans to appease the gods of old. That is what the old legends say. Now, the locals sell the story to tourists that, on certain nights, if you are very lucky, you can spot a woman covered in a bloody shroud, wandering around the Pits, wailing, looking for a lost baby or some such nonsense."

"That's the nonsensical part?"

"Of course. Stories of ghost mothers looking for lost babies are the oldest chestnuts in the world. I have another theory."

"You do?"

"Oh, yes. These screams are not of ancient sacrifices, no. The screams are from people taken, some of them centuries ago, and forced into servitude in the Court of Oberon, King of the Fairies. More to the point, their nefarious deeds continue to this very day. I have proof." Mr. Todd nodded as he pulled out a newspaper article from his jacket pocket. "It was what attracted Mr. Holmes to help me. This is one of a recent account. See? A man and woman went missing just a few weeks ago very near the Shrieking Pits. Gone! Vanished without a trace. We can help them as well as all the others kidnapped in the years gone by. Time runs differently there, you see. What passes as a day there counts as decades of years here. Do you see? While hundreds of years have passed here, many of those poor souls are still waiting to be set free. If we can only understand the science and mechanics of these portals, we could free them. Don't you see? It's so very obvious to anyone who can see!"

I cleared my throat and nodded, not so much in agreement but in an effort not to raise up any more emotion about something that the young man was so obviously passionate. I spared a glance at Mrs. Dowell, to gauge her reaction. She was calm, placid almost to the point of boredom. Yet, there was something in her eyes, something heavy and sad, as if she were holding back something. I wondered what that might be and made a mental note to ask her about my suspicions in the future.

I took a closer look at the newspaper article Mr. Todd had handed over to me during his rant. It was clipped out of The

Examiner, a local paper in Norfolk. The entire incident barely rated more than three paragraphs, scarcely a column's worth of ink. A local couple, Mr. Christopher Benson and his fiancée, Jocelyn Whitwell had gone on a picnic and never returned. A sudden elopement? That would be the most logical guess, but then, Mr. Todd was not the most logical of men.

"You know for certain that this was where they had stopped? Was there a blanket or basket?"

"No." Mr. Todd shook his head. "My guide assured me it was where the locals and adventurous tourists go to..." The young man blushed. "To picnic."

"Ah, I understand. To picnic? An out of the way place, is this? Private? Far from prying eyes?"

"Yes," Mrs. Dowell said. "I think you see the point, Dr. Watson."

"Oh, and how could I forget!" Mr. Todd scrambled in his inner jacket pocket and pulled out a small, silver coin. "There was this. I found it near where they had picnicked."

I took the coin and looked it over. It was about the size of a penny but looked to be pure silver. There were faded scratches around the edges like writing and in the center was a faded image of something with wings. A bird? An angel? I had seen ancient Roman coins, found along the banks of rivers, exhibited at the Royal Museum. None were this detailed. Or silver.

"Silver is a holy metal," Todd said. "It is prized by fairy folk."

"Is it?"

"According to some stories," Mrs. Dowell spoke up. "Others say gold is the favorite."

Todd's head turned towards her with a snap. "Nevertheless, I found the coin near the Benson and Whitwell kidnapping site and

Mr. Holmes thought it was incredible. 'Excellent!' was his exact word." Todd's enthusiasm suddenly dampened. "If I only knew what was to come. I swear, Doctor Watson, on my life, if I had only known I would have dragged him away from there, kicking and screaming! It kills me, pains me to the core, to know that he is now one of those forsaken souls, beyond our help, trapped forever in the world of the Fae."

"What exactly happened?" I said trying to take control of the conversation. "Tell me, exactly when did he go missing?"

"It was after we found the coin. We did a bit more investigating, looking over the land, tracking down magnetic anomalies." He pulled out a round silver box and flipped open the top. It was a compass, a beautiful piece of work in brass nestled in blue velvet. "It's a poor man's electrospectrascope but it's far more portable."

"An electrowhat?"

"It's a device Mr. Todd bought in Manhattan," Mrs. Dowell explained, "from a down on his luck Serbian."

"He is a brilliant scientist! His work is decades ahead of his peers. If you'd only take the time to read his papers or talk to him you'd change your mind!"

"Talk to him? He got nauseated because I have pierced ears! The man is a lunatic!"

I clapped my hands sharply and they both sat up like errant schoolchildren. "I'm sorry that I asked. Let's stay focused on the task at hand. Please, pray, continue."

"I was using this to track magnetic anomalies, whilst Mr. Holmes just meandered around, looking at God only knows what. Sometimes, he seemed more interested in the birds in the sky, the creek bed and the abandoned barn than anything else."

"Ah, I see." I made a mental note to look for the barn. "And then what happened. No, let me guess." I templed my hands, as

I'd seen my friend do so many times before and attempted to smile satirically. "He suggested you all go to dinner, to celebrate your discovery and he never made it to the restaurant. Am I correct?"

"Yes." Mrs. Dowell looked at me quizzically. "How did you know?"

"A typical Holmes maneuver." I shook my head at the memory of all the times I was sent on 'important life or death errands' only to find it was merely a ruse to keep me out of the way so he could go on some foolhardy investigation alone. Or to save my life.

"I wanted to contact the police then, but Bernadine convinced me to wait until morning. Not that it would've made any difference. No earthly force could have saved him by then, I fear."

"Hmm. No sign of him at all? He hadn't gone to his room? The concierge at the desk didn't see him?"

"No. We were the last humans to see him, Dr. Watson, I am certain of that."

"And you believe it was during the night that," I could feel my face flush as I said the words, "the fairies took Holmes?"

"Oh, yes." Ulysses K. Todd nodded, his eyes clear and his voice solid with certainty. "Of that I am quite convinced."

"But why do you think he was taken? Why did they not take you or Mrs. Dowell?"

"The court of Oberon takes only the most beautiful and best of the human folk they can find." Todd tapped his orthopedic shoe on the floor. "My burden is obvious. Mrs. Dowell is... how to put this discreetly? Not pure of blood."

Mrs. Dowell's jaw clenched, but she did not say a word in protest.

"But still, I don't understand. Why take Sherlock Holmes?"

Todd laughed. "What better prize to grace the court of Oberon than Sherlock Holmes?"

In as much as I knew my friend would revel in the compliment that he would warrant such attention from ethereal royalty, I still needed to understand more of what had happened. And, more pressing in my mind, why such a case would warrant any validity in the eyes of Sherlock Holmes. I did have one very unpleasant suspicion. A terrible card I was hesitant to play.

"Tell me, Mr. Todd. Where did you meet with Mr. Holmes? Here in London or did he meet up with you in Almertune?"

"He asked for us to come around to Baker Street at our earliest convenience. Unfortunately, I was ill." Mr. Todd's face went pale for a second and I worried I would need to get him a shot of brandy. "I wasn't able to keep that appointment. Mrs. Dowell went in my stead."

"Oh, that must've been an interesting engagement. Tell me, how did he seem to you?"

She arched her brow. "Seem?"

"What were your impressions when you first met Mr. Holmes?"

"Well, if the state of his apartment was any reflection of the man, he was a nervous wreck. There was a heavy, oily cloud hanging in the air and the place reeked of tobacco. I could smell it on my clothes for days afterwards. Trays of food sat untouched on the table. Papers and assorted periodicals littered the floor as if a typhoon had ripped through."

"Oh, well, that tells me very little. The flat was always like that. How did he appear health wise? Did he seem well rested? At peace?" I licked the tip of my pencil. "Sane?"

"He was pale, very thin, as if he had not been eating although the plates were filled with food. He was very excitable, strangely enough. There was a sparkle in his eye that belied his wan complexion."

"As I feared." I made a note in my book to look for his syringe. "Did he say why he wanted to go to Almertune? Any clue as to what he was hoping to find that was so tantalizing that it would pull him out of Baker Street?"

She shook her head. "No, sir. Nothing. He just said this was an excellent chance to get London out of his lungs for a while.

And considering the atmosphere, I couldn't agree more. So, after a very brief chat, I gave him his train ticket, the name of the hotel and some literature on the history of Almertune and the legends of the Shrieking Pits. Oh, wait... yes, he did have one request. He asked me for one more thing that took me a while to find. I'm surprised I forgot about it; it was very hard to track down. But in all the excitement since, it hardly seems relevant now."

I leaned forward in earnest interest. "What, pray tell?"

"He wanted maps. He asked for topographical ones and any that showed local river ways, docks and shipping routes near Almertune. I remember he was very apologetic when asking me to do this task, saying he usually had help that did all the busy work for him, but his assistant was off on holiday."

I pressed down so hard that I broke the tip of my pencil. "Ah. Does he?"

"Yes. I finally found the maps and had them delivered to Baker Street. We didn't see him again until we met in Almertune two weeks ago."

"Thank you," I said, closing my notebook. "I see you have Holmes' luggage?"

"Yes," Todd said. His enthusiasm from a moment ago had drained away into grief. "We thought it was appropriate to return it to you. I didn't know if he had any relations."

My mind turned to Mycroft Holmes, but I decided to keep it to myself for the time being unless it became important. "Let's take a look at what's inside, shall we?"

Mr. Todd laid it on my desk. It was an impeccable leather valise of a dark rich walnut hue with brass buckles and handles. It was beautiful, a piece of art. Mary had chosen it for him as a Christmas gift only three years ago. Upon opening it, I found several pieces of clothing still neatly folded, toiletries and a notebook filled with his curiously tight handwriting. I thumbed through it and a folded piece of paper fell out. I picked it up, the strong smell of lemons emanated from it. Upon opening, I found the sheet was blank. I refolded it and replaced it back in the journal. Digging through the clothing, I searched for the cursed syringe case. Instead, I found a small suede bag, cheap and tattered, with a bloody thumbprint marked on the front, cinched closed with a leather cord. There was something small but heavy inside it. I opened it and a coin slid out into my hand. It was a silver coin almost exactly like the one Todd had found at the Shrieking Pits.

"Oh... my... stars," Mrs. Dowell gasped.

"He already had a fairy coin?" Todd's eyes bugged at the sight. "But how?"

"The answer to that lies in one place, my lad." I slipped the coin back into the leather pouch and put it in my coat pocket. I called for Violet to retrieve my hat and coat and told her of my plans. She tutted and muttered something about dinner going to waste and the three of us were off to 221b Baker Street.

CHAPTER FOUR

DISCOVERY AT BAKER STREET

A distraught Mrs. Hudson met us on the doorstep of 221B Baker Street. She was impeccably dressed, solid and true, but her red-rimmed eyes and wrung out handkerchief told another story.

"Is it true, what I've read in the papers, Doctor Watson? Oh, tell me if you know anything about our dear Mr. Holmes! I've even approached his dreadful brother, Mycroft, and he wouldn't give me the time of day. And Scotland Yard doesn't even seem to care! With all he's done for them. It's a crying shame! Please, Dr. Watson, I am at my wit's end with worry."

I shuffled her inside, making introductions as we went. "I'm afraid I don't know anything new, Mrs. Hudson, but Mr. Todd and Mrs. Dowell and I are doing our best to get to the bottom of this mystery. We need to see his rooms."

"Please, do what you wish. You know where he hid his spare key." Mrs. Hudson covered her face with her handkerchief and wept. "Please, Doctor Watson, my heart can't take another Reichenbach!"

My stomach dropped at the memory of that dark time. I could still smell the crisp Alpine air and hear the roar of the waterfall. For three years, I lived under the weight of the false belief that Sherlock Holmes had died there, grappling with his nemesis,

Professor Moriarty, until they both fell to the bottom of the Reichenbach Falls. I remembered that burden all too clearly and had no desire to take it onto my shoulders again.

"Don't despair, Mrs. Hudson, the game is not over. Not yet!"

I took off, mounting the stairs two at a time as I ran up to the door to my old apartment. Mr. Todd and Mrs. Dowell scrambled up behind me. Their youth did nothing to keep up with my sheer determination. I found the key in its hiding place above the door frame and let myself in.

It had been two weeks since Holmes had left his apartment, but the presence of the man still hovered in the air. It wasn't just the thick, oily smell of that horrible shag tobacco he favored. No, it was more. There was an impression, a ghost of the man, imprinted on every wall. I half expected him to burst out from his bedroom, barely dressed, oblivious to all of us, with his prominent nose hooked inside a book. I could almost hear a violin playing in the room beyond. Oh, the hours of sleep I lost trying to drown out his infernal violin! The kitchen was a laboratory of beakers and Bunsen burners. The smells coming from there did nothing to whet the appetite. I could close my eyes and see him, holding a beaker over a flame, his eyes growing in excitement as the liquid inside bubbled and changed colors. "Eureka, Watson! I have found it!" I could see him saying, giddy as a schoolboy, "The answer to the puzzle!"

To open my eyes to an empty apartment took my breath away. The heaviness of the physical absence of Sherlock Holmes in 221B Baker Street seemed unreal, not possible.

"Doctor Watson?" Mrs. Dowell put her hand on my shoulder. "Are you all right?"

Her gentle touch brought me back to my senses and I nodded. "I'm fine. Let's get to work, shall we?"

As we entered the flat, I went over to open a window. It took a few good tugs before it would even budge an inch upward.

Holmes rarely opened the windows. He was never one for fresh air or whatever it was that passed for air that reeked off a London street. I looked down on Baker Street and watched people walking by, completely unaware of me watching them. It gave me a sense of impropriety, as if I was glimpsing what they would not want me to see. I have to admit, it was a bit of a thrill. I wondered to myself if Holmes ever felt such an emotion. Although, considering his analytical state of mind, the answer to that would be a resounding no. People were merely walking puzzles begging to be solved. He never attached any sort of raw feeling to the game. The only thrill I supposed he got from his view was intellectual at best.

I wondered what he would have made of the sparse pickings down below. There wasn't much to choose from. I spied a lanky man standing by a gaslight looking up at me. Alongside him was a stockier friend who also turned to look up at my window. Probably just curious readers of the Strand, I supposed. Holmes, of course, would have deduced their entire life stories within seconds. It was all a game to him, really. Humanity. From this window, he would have picked out a seaman on holiday, or a nanny stepping out with her lady's husband. I caught myself smiling at that thought. In spite of what he professed, Holmes' thoughts often trailed off to the lurid.

"Good Lord!" Mr. Todd exclaimed. "This place has been ransacked!"

"No, this is very much the normal state of things."

I looked around the chaos that Holmes called home. The general layout was as I had so often seen it. As one entered the room, to the right there was a chemist table where Holmes did his experiments. Along the wall, there were bookcases and Holmes' private desk, his wastebasket (full as always) and a cupboard beside it, stacked with dirty dishes. As one continued round the room, there was a fireplace, the hearth of Baker Street. Above the mantle, I could see a collage of maps, photographs and notes taped or, in some instances, nailed into the wall. I grimaced as I thought of what Mrs. Hudson would say to that. My comfortable ball and claw leather wing chair, into the seat of which I had worn quite a groove, sat across from Holmes' favorite French sofa settee, on which he lounged while smoking and thinking. On the floor, between our two chairs, there was a pile of papers and books, as if in a circle. And on top of one of the books, Holmes' black clay pipe. The one he preferred to smoke while thinking. It was a nest! Oh, I could see it now, Holmes sitting there, on the floor, smoking that blasted pipe and staring up at the mural on the wall, piecing together strings that I had yet to even see!

"I don't know what you think we'll find here in all of this hodgepodge," Todd said as he dragged his cane through a pile of papers.

"Mr. Todd, please! I must demand that you stop moving things. You are destroying what could be vital evidence."

"What evidence? There are papers strewn around and books."

"To investigate, Mr. Todd, one must preserve the scene." I sat down in the middle of what I called 'the nest', crossed my legs and made myself as comfortable as I could. "That is the very first lesson Holmes ever taught me."

Mrs. Dowell froze in her tracks. "Are you saying that a crime has happened here, Dr. Watson?"

"I don't believe that to be the case, no, but to figure out how the fairy coin came into his possession, for what reason he needed all those maps and to finally understand why Holmes agreed to go to Almertune, we need to see what he saw-before he left. Please, find a place to sit and be quiet. I need to concentrate."

I heard the rustle of Mrs. Dowell's dress as she took a seat behind me at Holmes' desk. Mr. Todd did not take her lead and wandered in front of me, obstructing my view of the collage.

"Is that it?" he said, putting his hands on his hips. "It's just a mish-mash of papers, pictures and maps. Look! There's even different colored twine running from one pushpin to another, zig zagging all over the place. What does it mean?"

"I don't know but, if you would please step aside, I'll decipher it."

The young man turned on his heel. "*You?*"

"Yes, *me*." I did my best to control my temper, which was slowly boiling over at the young man's impertinence. "I am the only one here trained in his methods and I alone understand how his mind works." I knew Holmes would laugh at that impetuous boast, but I soldiered on. "Now, if you would, please, sit down!"

"Ulysses, please," Mrs. Dowell coaxed the young man. "Let the man get on with his work."

Todd muttered something and shuffled off to sit behind me. I took a deep breath and pushed them both out of my mind. I forced my mind to be open and to actively *observe,* and not just lazily *see,* what was right in front of me. I had seen Holmes do this a hundred times, a thousand times! Even though he often assured me it was no trick, nothing superhuman, I began to doubt his word as I stared up at the mural above the mantel.

Newspaper clippings of the couple that went missing at the Shrieking Pits. He had circled their names and written the word *BIRDS* in the sideline.

Photographs. So many photographs of simple things. Just places and people along Baker Street. Strange. They were scattered over to the side, as if an afterthought.

There were maps. Topographical maps of Almertune, alongside another map showing the shipping routes and docks nearby. Four different colored twine, red, black, green and red, marked routes that all started near the Shrieking Pits but broke out towards different shipping docks. Something being exported? Imported? I didn't have a clue.

I looked around me at what made up Holmes' nest. There were several books. Two books on Vikings, a book on blacksmithing, one on Celtic legends and two more on fairies. In one of the books on Vikings, I found an envelope from the Diogenes Club used as a bookmark. The stationary inside was blank but scented. Lemons? Curious. Scattered around me were shipping logs, financial sections showing stock market values, local newspapers from Almertune and nearby counties, all of them well read with articles circled or torn out and added to the collage on the wall. I could imagine Holmes sitting there, his pipe billowing out foul smoke as he read each thing, gleaning facts that eluded me.

I shifted, trying to find a more comfortable position, and perhaps a new perspective, when I felt a sudden stabbing in my posterior. I reached behind me and felt something sharp, hidden in a pile of papers. I pulled it out. It was a fairy made of tin. There was a loop of fishing line out of the top of its head. A Christmas ornament? I hung it from my finger and let it flitter in the breeze. I stood up and walked over to the mantle. I looked up to the maps and then back to the tin fairy.

"How does this all fit?" I wondered aloud.

"The reason he came to Almertune is obvious," Mr. Todd said, coming over to me and taking the fairy from me. He twisted the loop of fishing line between his thumb and forefinger causing the tin fairy to twirl. "To help me to investigate the fairy abductions. Look at the map! I understand now. All the strings lead to the Pits! Exactly where I said the portal would be found!"

"I'm sorry, my good man, but it will take a lot more than a coin and a Christmas toy to convince me that the Sherlock Holmes I know would leave his precious London to go as far as Norfolk on a fairy hunt!" My eyes stopped on his desk; the drawer closed firmly shut. My heart grew heavy. "At least not in his right mind."

I stood up and bounded over to his desk. "If I could ask you to move, Madam?" She nodded, moved aside. I opened the drawer and removed the syringe case. I opened it. Empty! I slammed the drawer shut. "Damn!"

"What's wrong?" asked Mrs. Dowell.

I shook my head. The last thing I wanted the public to get wind of was my friend's unfortunate habits. "Mrs. Dowell, you said that Holmes was nervous, jittery, when you saw him here?"

"Yes."

"And in Almertune. Did he also exude those symptoms?"

"Symptoms? You make it sound as if he were sick."

"Poor choice of words, madam, but did he?"

"No. He actually seemed better once we settled in the hotel. More sharp, focused."

"I'm sure he did," I sighed. "Mr. Todd, are there many pharmacists in the village?"

Todd stammered. "Wh-why are you asking me?"

Good Lord, man, now is no time to play coy. I smelled the hashish on you back in my office."

The young man's shoulders slumped. "It helps with the pain of my scoliosis and my foot when it aches. And to help me sleep. My nerves...I am terribly hypersensitive."

"I'm not judging you, man! Just tell me if you were able to find a supply there."

Mrs. Dowell stepped forward. "I take special care of his supply, sir, if you have any questions, ask me. I can assure you that I never saw Mr. Holmes imbibe anything stronger than the local beer, Doctor Watson."

"I wish that allayed my fears, Mrs. Dowell but no, you wouldn't see, not if Sherlock Holmes doesn't want you to see."

All the fears I had pushed aside while on sabbatical came roaring back at me. In spite of the herculean effort it took to wean him off the horrible drug and my constant badgering him to preserve the marvelous gifts God had given him, he had begun using cocaine again.

I blamed myself. I should have seen the signs. He was bored, restless and completely at the end of his tether. And I left him alone in that state, knowing what he might do to avoid the mundane state of dull existence. I could only imagine that, in a state of cocaine induced psychosis, Holmes grabbed onto the lunacy of fairy abductions and had taken chase like a dog at the racetrack, running at breakneck speed after the metal rabbit. What had happened to him? Had he finally pushed his mind to the breaking point? Was he wandering around, lost and confused? Had his old habit returned stronger than ever, leading him to increase his usage beyond his original seven percent solution? Had it finally proved too much for his weakened system?

"What now, Doctor Watson?" Todd asked. He looked at me with pale, wounded eyes. Mrs. Dowell hovered close behind him, as if to catch him. I wanted to tell him it was not his fault, what had happened to Holmes. The blame rested entirely on my shoulders.

"Well, firstly, I should be glad I haven't had time to unpack," I said, trying to lighten the mood, if not for them but for myself. "Secondly, when is the next train to Almertune?"

CHAPTER FIVE

INTERRUPTED TRAIN RIDE

I made it back to my home in time to eat a cold dinner under my housekeeper's baleful eye. She was also none too happy to see me go off on another trip.

"Traveling is a dangerous tonic, Doctor Watson," Violet tutted as she folded and packed a new case of clean clothes. "It's none too healthy, I've always said. I believe that it is best to stay close to the hearth but, who listens to an old woman in spite of the fact she has never been sick a day in her life?"

"I do listen to you, my dear Violet, but unfortunately work calls me out." I rummaged through Holmes' carpetbag for anything that might be helpful and remembered his journal. I'd only thumbed through it briefly before and hadn't taken time to properly read it. There might be some sort of clue I had missed, so I tossed it into my case. "I just hope we find Holmes in one piece and in good health."

"Oh, I'm sure you will, Doctor Watson." Violet angrily snapped my case shut. "That man has as many lives as a cat, he does."

"Ah, but even cats run out eventually."

I took a hansom to the train station and found Mrs. Dowell waiting for me outside. She had changed into a silk day dress with off-white satin brocade that was dotted with a colorful peacock feather motif. She wore a veiled hat that also had an array of peacock feathers in the brim. In spite of the veil, I could see faint dark circles underneath her eyes. Her posture was strained as if it took all her will to keep erect. She smiled and nodded when she saw me wave to her.

"Good evening, Dr. Watson," she said, warmly. "Have your given your luggage to the porter?"

"Yes. It is all sorted. Where is Mr. Todd?"

She pointed towards a wooden bench where her companion was sitting by only the loosest definition of the word. The only thing holding him up was the metal post beside him.

"What happened to him, pray tell? He was energetic as a squirrel only a few hours ago."

"Indeed." She nodded and grinned with thin, straight lips. "I insisted he take his treatment tonight since has been so lax about it for the past few days. I'm afraid it has left him a bit incapacitated. "

"So I see."

"It's all for the best, Dr. Watson, I assure you. I needed the respite as much as he did. Please follow me. I'll show you to our car."

Mrs. Dowell was miraculously able to procure us a private car on the late train. She had also telegraphed the hotel to acquire lodging for the three of us at a generous rate. She was a remarkable and able lady and I was quite looking forward to getting to know better on our three-hour ride to Almertune.

I helped Mrs. Dowell load a very clumsy Mr. Todd into our compartment. He flopped down across me from and the smell of hashish filled the cabin. He immediately fell into a stupor. I opened a window and fanned in some fresh air.

"I'm sorry for the, um, inconvenience, Dr. Watson." She loosened Todd's collar and adjusted a pillow against the wall for his head. "The past few days have worn his nerves down to a thread."

"He must have smoked quite a bit to put him in that state."

"Oh, no. He rarely has more than one cigarette. This is from the opiate I put in is tea."

"You medicated his tea?"

"Don't look at me like that. He hasn't slept in two days. It was the only way I knew he would get any rest at all."

"No judgment on my part, dear lady, none at all. Considering the source, I shouldn't expect anything less."

The flush in her cheeks was back. "What do you mean, 'the source'? Are you implying something because I am a woman? Or because I am of Japanese descent?"

"No, not at all! I meant because of your unconventional partnership with Mr. Todd here."

"Partnership? Let me get this very straight with you, Dr. Watson. There is no partnership." Her dark eyes bore into me and a sweat broke on my brow as I felt myself flush. "I am in the employ of his grandmother, Mrs. Eunicia Todd, an old fool, richer than God and who finances every whim her gadfly grandson sets his sights on. One day, we are traveling to Florida to look for skunk apes and the next we are tramping in the Badlands looking for thunder lizards. There is no 'relationship' here, Dr. Watson. I am paid to keep him alive."

"Yes, and you obviously do a very good job. And, let me commend you on your speech. You speak English fluently. I can hardly detect an accent at all."

"As well I should. I am a British citizen."

"Oh, really?"

She sighed. "My father was a diplomat who served in her Majesty's employ in Japan." Her eyes dulled and her voice went flat, as if she had told the story a thousand times. "There, he met my mother. After he fulfilled his term, they married and moved back to London. She died shortly after I was born. The English climate never agreed with her."

"Oh, well... yes."

"I spent my childhood traveling the world with my father."

"Oh, well, what stories you must have to tell. I'm sure you make an excellent traveling companion."

"I will have you know, Dr. Watson, I am more than a companion." The spark and snap came back to her voice as she spit out the words. "I speak three languages and write in five. I am fluent in shorthand and can type nearly 30 words a minute. I am also a certified nurse."

"Yes, well, that must come in handy considering the skunk apes..."

"I also fence, I am a crack shot and I am trained in ju-jitsu. I know several ways to break your arm from just where I am sitting. Is there anything else you need to know?"

"Married?"

"Widowed. Next question."

I tugged at my collar. "Do you need a drink as badly as I do?"

"Probably worse. Shall we try to find the dining car?"

"Yes, please."

As we stood to leave, two men blocked our doorway. One was squat, barrel-chested, with a well chewed cigar slammed in the crook of his mouth. He wore a bowler hat and heavy coat in spite of the warm weather. The other was taller and leaner with a sharp ferrety face. I recognized them as the two I saw looking up at me from Baker Street.

"Excuse me, sir," I said. "We need to pass."

The tall one shook his head and took a step forward, pushing Mrs. Dowell and myself back into the car. I kept her behind me, shielding her from the brutes as they both came in. The tall one jutted his jaw at me and pointed a burnt, blackened finger into my face. Every muscle in his arm was taut as if he were ready to strike out like a cobra. "Don't play games wit' me, brother. Where did he hide it, then? Eh? Where's the treasure? Where did that toerag hide it" he grunted.

I slapped his offending digit away from me. "Get out of my car, sir, before something drastic happens."

"Oy! It's not him!" the squat one shouted, pointing over at Todd. "That's him there! He's the one I saw with it!"

"Right!" The tall one pushed me aside and went for Todd, grabbing the sleeping man by his coat lapels, pulling him up to his feet and shook him awake.

"Where's the treasure?" he screamed into Todd's face. "Where is it? Where's the treasure?"

Todd blinked back at him with dull, dazed eyes. "W-w-w-what?"

"Talk, you thieving scum!" The thug threw Todd down onto the seat and punched the poor man in the face, bloodying his nose. "Talk! Or soon you won't have a mouth to talk with!"

"Leave him be!" I shouted and rushed towards the thug, but before I could get close enough to help Todd, the squat one pulled out a thick, knotty shillelagh club as long as his arm and slammed it into my gut. I felt my floating ribs crack and I folded in half and landed on the floor. I pulled myself to my knees, blackness whirling around my eyes as I tried to get my wind back.

The fat man pointed the club at Mrs. Dowell, "Now, you be a good girl, you hear? I wouldn't want to knock any of those pearly whites out of your head."

"Oh, I do think that would be ambitious of you." I heard her say and then I heard a few pops, a slap and the fat little man was on the floor beside me, quite unconscious.

I sat up in time to see her sidestep towards the tall man and strike out, taking his left hand with her left in one swift move, bending his thumb so it was lying alongside his forearm. I heard the snap of bone and the man screeched like a whelp, falling to the floor like a bag of wet sand.

"Arrrrgh! You she-devil!"

Her left hand kept a painful grip on the screaming man as her right hand reached under her fitted vest and pulled out a brushed silver double barreled, rosewood handle derringer. She pressed it against his forehead. "Listen carefully." Her voice was soft and so, so cold. She cocked the slender hammer back with her thumb. "When I release you," She twisted his arm for emphasis, "you will take your partner over there and you will leave. Be quick about it. I'd hate for my finger to suddenly slip. Does that sound like an agreeable plan?"

The man's blood shot eyes widened, and he nodded emphatically.

"Wonderful. So good doing business with you." She released his left hand and he scrambled like a crab towards his friend. He kicked at the fat man until he regained consciousness and then they both skedaddled away out the door.

"Dr. Watson? If you can, would you please make sure that they have gone?"

"Should I call a porter?"

"If you can find one. It's been my experience that at this time of night they are usually too drunk to be of much use anyway."

I nodded numbly and, holding my ribs and bruised pride, took a few steps outside our car. I spied two porters in dark suits standing nearby. I called out them.

"Did you see two men just now? They accosted me and my friends in our car 27. One is a short man with a shillelagh and the other taller, with a broken thumb."

One porter tipped his hat. "Don't worry, Dr. Watson, We'll see to it," he said and they left together.

I went back to our car, closed and locked the door. Mrs. Dowell holstered her derringer beneath her fitted vest and attended to Todd, cleaning up his face with a handkerchief.

"Is he injured?"

"Just a bloody nose, nothing broken. Poor devil has fallen asleep. I doubt he'll remember anything, but he will feel it in the morning." She pulled a silver and burgundy blanket down from the overhead storage and covered him with it, tucking him in like a child. She sat down beside him, exhausted. She unbuttoned the top three buttons of her vest, took her hat off and unfurled her hair, letting it fall down on her shoulders in waves. She ran her fingers through it, untangling stray knots. The sudden familiarity was a bit uncomfortable, I will admit, as a gentleman and a widower, but after our unfortunate encounter, I suppose she saw me more as a brother in arms. Or perhaps she simply was too tired to be confined by social restrictions. Either way, I am not ashamed to admit, here in my writing, that I found Mrs. Bernadine Dowell more and more fascinating.

"I'm afraid have to postpone our drink, Dr. Watson. I can't leave him alone, unprotected."

"Agreed. What do you think they meant?" I sat across from her, grimacing as every rumble of the train ran through me. "The treasure? Did they mean the coin?"

She shrugged, her eyes closing. "One coin does not a treasure make."

"I suppose that depends on the coin. Either way, it looks like our adventure has begun earlier than I'd expected."

"So far, in my life, I've found that there is one thing I can count on," Mrs. Dowell said, yawning, "and that is adventure never sticks to a schedule."

She soon fell asleep, but I couldn't even dream of sleeping so I stayed awake and stood watch over my new friends. Mrs. Dowell was becoming more and more a most interesting companion. I couldn't help but smile remembering how she disposed of the thug. I made a mental note to ask her to teach me that move.

No other unpleasant visitors bothered us during our trip to Almertune. I sat and watched the shadowy scenery glide by and pondered over the few clues that I had found so far, jagged pieces to a puzzle that I could not snap together. Why were those maps pinned to his wall? What interest would a man like Sherlock Holmes, a man completely devoted to the realm of rationality and reason, have in a man as completely otherworldly as Ulysses K. Todd? My mind simply could not digest the ideas of fairies and Holmes in the same sentence. Was it some sort of snap in judgment due to his abominable cocaine use? And what of the coin in the blood smeared bag? I took it out of my pocket and looked at it in the dim gaslight. A dingy, cold slab of silver is all I saw. If it were magical, it did not live up to the mystique. Those thugs that roughed up Todd thought it was valuable. That worried me. What treasure did they think Todd had with him? And then a horrible thought dawned on me: Holmes, not Todd. What treasure did they think Holmes had? A sick feeling burned into the pit of my stomach. I feared my friend had got-himself into something far more dangerous that I had even conceived.

CHAPTER SIX

A DELIVERY AT DRAUGRHODD INN

It was nearing 2 a.m. when the train pulled into the station. I gently nudged Mrs. Dowell on the shoulder, whereupon her hand shot out and grabbed mine, twisting it.

"It's me! Dr. Watson!" I said, trying not to cry out in pain as I went to my knees. My ribs were still tender from the beating from a few hours ago.

"Oh!" She released me and shook her head. "I'm so sorry, Dr. Watson. You startled me. It was instinct."

"If that is so, then I pray never to startle you again. I just wanted to let you know we are here."

"Yes, thank you. Again, please forgive me. It's been a very long few days for me." She began wrapping her hair into a bun and putting on her hat. "I'll see to Ulysses."

I pointed to her unbuttoned blouse. "And..."

She blushed which was a delight to see in such a formidable female. "Thank you."

"I'll scout ahead to make sure our friends aren't waiting somewhere for us."

"A sound plan."

When I returned, Mrs. Dowell and Mr. Todd were both ready to depart. She looked stunning, as if she had just stepped out of a salon. He looked slightly bewildered, gently touching his swollen nose. "There wasn't any sign of them anywhere. I even waited

outside to see if I could spot them leaving but no such luck. It is as if they disappeared into thin air."

"Perhaps they did," Todd said, grinning. "Perhaps they were emissaries?"

Mrs. Dowell rolled her eyes, but I decided to take the bait. "From whom, pray tell?"

"The Fairy Court, of course! To retrieve the coins. We must get back to the village!" He pushed by me and started out the door. "While the trail is hot!"

"I thought you said he wouldn't remember?" I asked Mrs. Dowell.

"I'd hoped that he wouldn't," she sighed and made a sweeping gesture to the door. "Shall we go? Before he gets too far ahead and we end up having to find him as well."

We retrieved our luggage with little problem and with still no sign of the thugs that approached us only a few hours before. I was amazed at how they had vanished. A part of me began to wonder if Mr. Todd might be more on target than I thought.

Mrs. Dowell had arranged for a hansom cab to be waiting for us to take us to the oddly named Draugrhodd Inn. The landlord had kindly informed Mrs. Dowell that he'd kept in reserve the rooms they had stayed at during their recent stay with Holmes. I would be in the room he had stayed in, which served my purposes well indeed.

"Odd name for a hotel. What does it mean?"

Todd rubbed his hands together. "Oh, it is just another piece of the puzzle, Dr. Watson. The Draugr is a ghost that guards treasure and devours anyone that tries to steal from the hoard. Hodd, see? It's Old English or some derivative."

"Norwegian, actually, Old Norse," Mrs. Dowell broke in. "It means 'the again walker' or 'one who walks after death'."

"Impressive, Mrs. Dowell," I said. "You are turning out to be quite a treasure trove."

She smiled back at me. "Deciphering tongues are a specialty of mine."

"UGH! Old English, Old Norse, what does that matter?!" Todd interrupted. "What is important is that the link between the name of the oldest building in the village and the ghost that supposedly wanders around the Shrieking Pits. It shows an ancient link to something extraordinary and supernatural happening in Almertune. Or am I boring you both?" He slumped back in his seat and stared out the window, sulking, for the rest of the journey.

At first, I felt a desire to beg forgiveness from Mr. Todd but, frankly, my heart wasn't in it. I had done nothing wrong in complimenting his companion's intellectual prowess. In my mind, she was due an apology from him for his utterly childish display. The more I thought about it, the colder my heart turned towards the odd young man who had pulled me into this mystery. And, if all were to be said aloud, my heart grew warmer for the woman who endured his employ. Still, he was the key to where Sherlock Holmes had disappeared and, so far, my only lead to finding him and, in the best of all possibilities, alive.

The ride was only thirty minutes or so into the town. I pulled up the shade to take in the scenery but in the gloom before dawn, it was a fool's errand. The only things I could make out were dark shapes and ominous shadows passing by. I recalled what Holmes had said about the apprehension he found when traveling in rural communities. He said evil was more apt to grow in places where houses were spread so far apart, where honest eyes to watch against it were few and far between. I suspect that is why he rarely strayed far from the urban sprawl of London. While he might endure a stroll through pastoral grounds to ease my constant worry about his health, I think open spaces were abhorrent to him. So many things could happen in secret in such places. Violence unnoticed, screams unheard. A stone thrown into a pond would sink with barely a ripple. Perhaps that would be the case for a common man, but not Holmes. It was inconceivable to me that someone with the force of personality of Sherlock Holmes could fade away without leaving behind some kind of trace. Impossible, I told myself, if only to keep my own fears of never finding him at bay.

The cab pulled up in front of the Inn. It had a formidable exterior, roughly hewn rock and wood. Ivy and honeysuckle intertwined around the front door and battled for dominance. I could see why it had weathered the centuries. But, because of the dark, I could see little else of the village.

We were met by Mr. Eric Donnelly, the landlord, a tall man, very broad in the shoulder and red faced.

"Mr. Todd and Mrs. Dowell. You've returned at last!" He greeted our party with open arms and so much enthusiasm that the sheer blast at such an early hour caused me to draw away. "And a new companion, I see!" He took my hand and shook it like a dog with a bone. "Let's hope he doesn't go the way of your last one! HAHAHA!"

My feelings towards this man instantly hardened.

"This is Dr. John Watson," said Mrs. Dowell. "A friend of the missing Mr. Holmes."

"Oh, apologies, sir! I suppose you're here to sort out the mystery as well, eh? Come in, come in!" He waved us inside. The foyer was decorated like a hunting room. Trophies of boar and deer hung on the dark oak wall beside oil paintings of foxes being pursued by men in powdered wigs on horseback. The blood red plush rugs on the floor completed the motif. Beside the registry desk was a door that led to a dining room. Across the room was a closed door that led to who knew where. A kitchen perhaps? Or, if the landlord was indeed trying to put on a gentrified air, a library full of leather-bound books that were never read. A staircase ahead of us led to the rooms upstairs.

"Boy! Take their bags to their rooms."

A surly teenage lad of about seventeen came from behind the register and lurched himself towards our bags. "I have a name," I heard him say, "If you ever remembered to use it."

The landlord gave him a hard-sideways glance but kept his smile bright and plastered to his face. His eyes remained hard as onyx as he watched the lad manhandle our bags up the stairs. "I am so happy to have you back as a guest, Mr. Todd! I kept your rooms exactly as you requested. Although I would be remiss if I didn't say I had a devil of a time keeping them open for you and your guests. What with all the tourists that are flooding into town and all."

"Tourists?" Todd shook his head. "What tourists? Last week you were complaining about the lack of paying guests. You even said you were afraid the inn was going broke and might go the way of the rest of the village."

"Well, that was before, wasn't it? Before the great Sherlock Holmes went and got himself missing right out there in our very own famous Shrieking Pits! Now, the house is filled to the brim. I'm turning people away like vermin!"

"Is that so? And who might be interested in that?" I did my best to keep my face completely neutral as I glanced around, half expecting to see the thugs from the train.

"Oh! We have people coming from all sorts of places to try and figure out the mystery! Some are just busybodies and amateur detectives. I've had a dickens of a time keeping that room empty, I don't mind telling you. I could've made a pretty penny if I'd been at leisure to let it out." Mr. Donnelly looked directly at Mrs. Dowell. "I even had a group of actual supernatural investigators all the way from London try and pay me double for a look at the Holmes Suite.""You will be compensated, I assure you. Add the expense to our bill." Mrs. Dowell signed her name into the ledger. "You know where to send it."

"Thank you kindly, ma'am. I do appreciate it."

"W-wait a minute," I stammered. "The *Holmes* Suite?"

"Oh, yes, sir! Named after our late, famous benefactor, God rest his soul, wherever he is. That's where you'll be staying. It's next door to Mr. Todd and across from Mrs. Dowell. You are a lucky devil, if I may say so, sir. Most requested room in the house. OH! Before I forget, a box came for you, Mr. Todd. Something all the way from New York. It's heavy. I put it in your room, for safe keeping."

"Excellent! Yes! Everything is coming together. I can feel it!" Mr. Todd scooped up the keys from the desk, handed one to Mrs. Dowell and one to me and bounded up the stairs. "Oh, if we had only had it before Mr. Holmes was taken!"

"Ulysses!" Mrs. Dowell called after him. "You can open the box tomorrow. There are still a few hours of night left before sunrise. I suggest we use them to rest."

"Rest? Are you mad, woman?" He scrambled back downstairs, grabbed Mrs. Dowell by the shoulders and kissed her on the cheek. "I couldn't possibly rest now. With everything I've worked for so close to fruition! You wait and see, Dr. Watson! The veil is waiting to be broken. We will save your friend and all the others! Wait and see! And she wants me to rest? Can you imagine?"

"Come along, Ulysses." Mrs. Dowell took the young man by the arm and walked with him up the stairs. "I'll make you some tea."

The number on my key was 21B. I smirked at the coincidence. Holmes always said that only people with small minds never saw the miracle of coincidences. He believed that it was the little things that were, in the end, the most important. It was as far into the romantic as his mind ventured. Still, I imagine he would have chuckled as I did when I received the key.

I heard Mrs. Dowell and Mr. Todd arguing over the temperature of his tea as I passed by their rooms, and I started to chuckle when I came to dead stop in front of 21B. The door to

my room was slightly ajar. I nudged it open with my foot, my fists clenched in case the thugs from the train had decided to bring the fight here.

I was relieved to find only the young porter slinging my luggage onto my bed. I relaxed and smiled at the young man as I handed him a tip. "Thank you. I'm sorry, I didn't catch your name."

He stopped for a second as if surprised to be seen. "Oh. I'm Colin. Colin Leerson."

"Leerson? I was under the impression the landlord was your father."

"Stepfather." He spit out the word. "Married my mum a few years ago. Her family owned this house. We called it home for generations. It's the only thing worth having in this forsaken town. It was my future, see? My birthright and then Mr. Donnelly sweeps in, courts my mum and, before you know it, I'm suddenly a servant in my own house."

"You must have rights as the first-born son."

"You'd think so, wouldn't you?" His face darkened. "But, no. Me mum signed it all over to Donnelly. As a flipping wedding present. Can you believe it? Turned out her own child, she did, for the attentions of a husband. And a snake of one, at that! She died only a year ago and he's been courting every girl that comes near. And take it from me, that devil might have said he kept these rooms closed for you and your friends but he's a filthy liar. I happen to know that he took a pound or two from a few shady looking types so they could poke around in this very room."

"Why? What did they expect to find?"

Colin shrugged. "They didn't stay long. Just wanted a poke around the room where the famous Sherlock Holmes slept. It's sick, if you ask me, what this has all come to."

"I agree. It must be very trying for you."

He smiled and nodded, beaming at me, his co-conspirator against Mr. Donnelly. "Don't you worry. I'll make my fortune. And when I do, I'll buy back this place and set it all right."

"I wish you all the luck in the world, Mr. Leerson."

"By the way, did I hear them call you Dr. Watson? As in the Dr. Watson that writes all those Sherlock Holmes stories?"

"Yes, I am he." I fought to keep my voice calm. It was hard enough when Holmes referred to my work as fiction but to hear a stranger refer to my essays as stories, it made me bristle. "However, what I write are actual accounts of adventures I have had with my friend, Sherlock Holmes. They are not fiction. Not in the least!"

"No offense meant, sir, I was just making sure I had the right man for a business proposal." He pulled out a small envelope. "Would you be interested in a special delivery that came for Mr. Holmes?"

I reached for it, but he pulled it just out of my grasp. "How did you come by it?"

"One of the perks of working the front desk. Unfortunately, I never had a chance to give it to him before... well, before he vanished. Still, I thought it might be of interest, to the right party."

"And by party, you mean buyer."

Colin shrugged. "How else do you expect a young man can buy back his birthright?"

My heart hardened against this young man just as much as it had against his stepfather. We haggled and finally settled on a price, a hefty one especially for a retired doctor living on a soldier's pension. He handed over the envelope.

"It's been opened."

Colin shrugged, "Didn't make much sense anyhow," he said and bid me goodnight.

I followed him to the door and might have closed the door a tad bit harder than necessary.

Sitting on my bed, I opened the envelope and found inside a blank sheet of paper. I looked at the paper, tried to gauge its thickness and origin the way Holmes would do. I smelled it for no other reason than I had seen Holmes do the same. It had the same strange lemony smell. I held it over the oil lamp to see if there was a watermark and suddenly, letters bloomed on the page.

S.H.

Don't engage.

It was signed:

M.H.

I was confounded at the meaning of the message. I shook my head and tossed it on my bedside table. I must admit that many of my fears for my friend evaporated at the inclusion of Mycroft Holmes into the equation. If his brother was involved in this mystery, then I knew that it wasn't some drug induced mania that had brought Holmes to this mad fairy hunt. He was obviously here on business for Mycroft, some sort of underhanded shenanigans that only the Diogenes Club would get mixed up in.

The Diogenes Club! That triggered something deep in my sleep deprived brain. There was something... something. An envelope! Yes!

I dug into my luggage, found Holmes' journal and turned it over, shaking it until a white linen envelope fell onto my bed. The Diogenes Club stamp was there in the left-hand corner. I pulled out the blank piece of stationary and examined it. The faint smell of lemons stung my nose. I could see nothing in the dim light of my room, so I held it over the gas lamp for more illumination.

AH! Right before my eyes, words began to form as the heat from the lamp activated the lemon juice used for ink.

Dearest Brother,

Yes! The coin is the last piece of the puzzle! Your talent for legwork, as always, in invaluable to Her Majesty. Continue onward and report once you know the whereabouts of the treasure. A knighthood for you if all comes about as planned!

As always,

M.H.

Again, talk of a treasure but what sort of treasure hunt did Mycroft send his brother on that would end in a knighthood? And then a second reply to a message sent from Holmes to his brother with only two words. My blood chilled at the meaning. It was a warning. Don't Engage. Engage in what? What nefarious plot had Mycroft sent his brother into unawares? I had only a scarce idea of what politics and plots the members of the Diogenes Club played at and, for the first time, I suddenly longed for the misguided idea that this was all just one of Holmes' drug binges.

I stumbled, half aware, through my nighttime toiletries. I scarcely remember lying down to sleep, my head so aflame with dark possibilities. Exhaustion from the trip and all that had befallen me in the past twenty-four hours crashed down on me. Sleep was far from restful. I had dreams, foggy, disjointed dreams where I could hear Holmes crying out to me for help but everywhere I turned, I was stopped by a shrieking, bloody ghost, grabbing at me with her needle sharp nails. I would turn and run, looking frantically for Holmes only to find a pile of silver coins. I ran my fingers through them and they fell from my hands, melting into a silver mush that morphed into the shrieking woman who clutched me by my throat, strangling me, all the while Holmes' screams grew louder and louder inside my head.

CHAPTER SEVEN

PIECES TO THE PUZZLE

I was grateful when a loud, sharp, knocking on my door woke me from my nightmare. I heard Todd shouting, "Dr. Watson! Dr. Watson! Wake up! Let me in! Let me in before they see me!"

I ran to the door without even a dressing robe and let the poor fool in before he bashed the door down.

"To one side!" Todd said as he rushed in, pushed me aside, slammed the door shut and threw himself against it. He was wearing rumpled clothes, obviously the same suit he had on yesterday. He clutched to his chest the most remarkable screened box, constructed from polished dark walnut. It had gleaming brass tubes jutting out of the top and on the front were three dials. "You mustn't let them in!"

"Who? What in the world are you jabbering about, man?"

Suddenly, there was a pounding at the door. "Todd! I know you are in there! You can't keep it to yourself!"

Todd looked at me with eyes doubled in size from fright. He shook his head back and forth and mouthed the words, "No!"

I pushed him to the side, grabbed the doorknob and opened the door. Three very surprised looking academic type fellows stared back at me in shock. I must have looked a fright, standing there in my sleepwear, unshaven, my hair shaggy and uncombed. I shouted back in my roughest, drill sergeant voice, "Oi! What the hell do you think you're doing?! Be off with you before I call the landlord!"

They scampered away, mumbling apologies, nearly tripping over each other as they ran away down the stairs. I could scarcely contain my laughter before I closed the door behind me. Mr. Todd, meanwhile, did not see the humor.

"You almost let them in! What were you thinking?!"

"Oh, calm down. Seriously, I don't know what you were so afraid of. They ran away like scared field mice. Who were they, anyway?"

"Competitors. Rivals for membership into the LSPR."

"LSP what?"

"The London Society for Psychical Research! Good Lord, man!" Todd shook his head and nearly spit out the words. "Do try and keep up!"

I bit my tongue as I went to the vanity, poured water into the bowl and washed my hands and face. Todd loped around the room nervously; his clubbed foot caused him to have a queer sort of gait, up and down, as if on a small ship in rough seas. He gripped the box tightly to his chest.

"Where is Mrs. Dowell?" I asked. "I have new information I need to share."

"She went out. She wanted to scout out the crowds or some such nonsense."

"Crowds?"

"Yes, crowds! Look out the window! While you were sleeping the morning away, the hordes have crashed in the front gates!"

I checked my pocket watch. It was barely 8 a.m. I don't call that exactly sleeping the day away but, obviously, maniacs kept different hours than a normal people.

I looked out the window.

The hotel was in a cul-de-sac and what I would call the town square was straight ahead. I didn't notice anything when we arrived early this morning because of the darkness but now, in the light of day, I could see that a festival had been laid out. There were booths, balloons and people, nearly a hundred or so milling around. Two little girls wearing brightly colored wings ran, squealing, away from their parents and toward a vendor selling cakes. I opened the window and could hear faint music from a band playing below.

Mrs. Dowell knocked on my door and walked in, fanning herself with a lace fan. She was wearing a simple pale green walking dress with delicate red piping along the bodice that highlighted the auburn in her hair. In spite of the heat, she looked as fresh as a spring shower.

"Good morning, boys! I'm glad to see you both up. I've been outside, scouting the area. They have turned a tragedy into a carnival. You have opened up a very lucrative and lurid can of worms, Ulysses."

"Me? I didn't start this." Todd sputtered and stopped his manic pacing. "It is puerile garbage. What does this have to do with my research?"

"Research? I don't give a damn about your infantile quest!" I felt a heated rage rising up from my gut. "I'm not here to help you in your insane hunt, Todd. I am here to discover what happened to my friend."

"But I thought we already discussed that, Dr. Watson. He was taken by the Fae to serve in the court of King Oberon. With my transponder, I can contact the Royal Court and work out a treaty to get our loved ones back!"

"No. Let me stop you right there, Todd. Perhaps others continue to do so," I glanced at Mrs. Dowell who stared back at me with steel in her eyes, "but I refuse to play the part of nursemaid to your absurd theories."

"Dr. Watson, perhaps we should talk outside." Mrs. Dowell reached out for my arm. "Please. Before you say anything else."

"No. He is an adult and deserves the truth."

"Ulysses, are you feeling well?" she asked Todd. "Perhaps you should go back to the room and have some tea."

"No." The young man held his box like a shield. "I am prepared to counter anything he says. I'm used to the wiles of skeptics and nonbelievers."

"Fine but, Dr. Watson, I beg you." She leaned in and whispered. "Be careful."

"Mr. Todd, I have proof here that Holmes did not accompany you to aid in your hunt for fairies. No, it pains me to tell you but this whole trip was a ruse. For what specific reason, I have no idea. All I can surmise so far is that he was on a mission for her Royal Majesty, sanctioned by his brother, Mycroft, under the guidance of the Diogenes Club."

"What is the Diogenes Club?" Mrs. Dowell asked.

"For all intents and purposes, it is a stodgy, elite gentleman's club."

"But it is actually a government office?"

"My dear, in many ways, the Diogenes Club is the government."

I pulled the blank sheet of paper from the journal and held it to the lamp until the letters once again appeared. Mrs. Dowell took the sheet and read it aloud as Todd cradled his box. "And then there is this special delivery message from Mycroft to Sherlock Holmes. It unfortunately did not arrive in time. Whatever was in the message Holmes sent to Mycroft, this was his response."

"It always comes back to that damned coin." She muttered.

"I know. I don't understand the entire puzzle yet, but somewhere out there is a treasure. Of what kind, I haven't the faintest idea. Perhaps more of these silver coins? Perhaps they are more valuable than we know. What I do know is that it has claimed three people, so far. That lunching couple," I counted off two on my fingers, "and Sherlock Holmes."

"If the Diogenes Club is a secret branch of the government, it does explain why Scotland Yard hasn't been investigating."

"Or has been investigating on the sly," I said. "I've never known a Scotland Yarder to give up a case very easily. I suggest we talk to the local constabulary, find out if anything new has come up."

"Good luck finding him. In a town this small, they probably trade shifts playing policeman."

"Either way, you have to admit that this all points to something very much on the earthly plane and not anything with wings."

"No." Todd shook his head as he rocked back and forth. "Nononono..."

Mrs. Dowell took a deep breath and put her hand on his shoulder. "Ulysses, look at this as a researcher. You have to agree that the evidence all points to..."

"Royalty. It all points to royalty." Todd stood up, the box held fast to his heart. "Queen calls out to King. That is what this is about: royalty." He dashed clumsily towards the door, saying, "I'll show you. With this electrospectrascope transponder, I'll prove it! Don't worry, Dr. Watson. I'll get Holmes back for you. I'll get them all back!" he cried out and slammed the door behind him.

"I'm sorry, Dr. Watson but I have to go after him before the damn fool hurts himself."

"I understand. Go and do what you must. I have a damn fool of my own to find.

CHAPTER EIGHT

'A FIGGERMENT OF THE IMAGINATION…'

I dressed and went downstairs hoping to get breakfast. The dining room was open and buzzing with activity. I was seated quickly, ordered tea, toast, and eggs. Looking around the room, I was astonished to find the lads I had scared away from my door only an hour ago at a table near the window. They were huddled together like conspirators, drawing marks on a map they had spread out on the table. One of them saw me and I nodded, amiably, and they quickly turned the other cheek, folded up their map and left. Colin angrily swooped in behind them and solemnly cleared their table, wiped it down and then disappeared back into the kitchen.

Behind me, I overheard a man griping about the weather. "It rained again this morning. Bah! That will erase any sort of physical evidence. Bah! I don't even know why we're here. The site is obviously too old for any true, scientific investigation." His friends nodded their heads in exasperation.

"Still, the beer is good."

"Bah!"

The table to the right of me sat a trio of women in black gauzy dresses and veils. They had a completely different take on the weather. "Isn't it auspicious, sisters? The morning rain? The ionic spike in the air will definitely vex the spirits into coming into play, don't you agree?" They all nodded and tittered, looking for all the world like crows in fancy dress.

"And you heard, sister, about the sighting?"

They tittered and cawed in excitement to such a pitch that I couldn't make out anything more. I turned and said, "Excuse me, ladies. Did I hear there was a sighting?"

"Yes! Yes!"

"Of what?" I asked, innocently.

"Of the Bloody Woman of the Shrieking Pit!" they all said in chorus. "The Bloody Woman was seen in the woods to the West."

"The West? But isn't the Shrieking Pit towards the East?"

They flittered their black lacey handkerchiefs as they all spoke at once.

"Yes! Yes!"

"Isn't it mysterious?"

"Never heard of a spirit change course, have we, sisters?"

"No, no!" They all said in a breathy chorus. "It is very... so very *mysterious*!"

I gave them my most practiced pleasant smile, bid them a good day and turned to dig into my breakfast. The company did nothing for my appetite, but I forced myself to eat anyway. I had enough experience with past adventures to know that I might not get another chance before the end of the day. The past few hours had given me ample evidence that I had no idea what to expect when I left the relative safety (if still insane) comforts of the hotel.

Stepping outside, my earlier worries solidified.

It was even madder outside.

When I was a boy, my grandmother told me stories about carnivals that were held only when the Thames froze over. They were called Frost Fairs. The last one was in 1814, when my Gran was just a girl of ten or so. She would regale us with vivid stories about how magical it was to see billowing tents with brightly colored streamers, hawkers walking up and down selling hot

chestnuts or cider, and festival rides like carousel horses and swings going full force in the middle of the Thames! Oh, and an elephant! How could I forget how her eyes would go wide when she retold us the story of when they walked an elephant across the frozen river.

The English winter has grown milder since my Gran's girlhood so her grandchildren never had the great fortune of ice skating from Tower Bridge to Blackfriar's Bridge as she had done. It was something I've always regretted, not being able to share in that piece of family lore.

However, standing here in the greenway of the tiny village of Almertune, sweltering in the heat of May, I believe I have glimpsed at least a sliver of what my Gran must have seen.

Right in front of me on the green, outside the Draughrhodd Inn, it was if a circus sprouted up like dandelions overnight. There were a dozen tents, maybe more, selling food, drink and novelty items I could barely describe. Some poor farmer had shackled up three ponies to a rotating pole, secured leather horns painted white onto their foreheads and was offering unicorn rides for three pence. I heard high pitched screams and turned to see a Traver Circular Swing precariously spinning and flinging a handful of young ladies, their skirts shamefully flapping in the breeze. The noise between the vendors in the booths shouting blended in with the screams of the rival hawkers.

Two of the hawkers set their sights on me. On the right side, was a tall man, in a mortician's mourning suit and top hat. He walked slowly, very dramatically, pounding his very large stick in the ground before him as he circled a crowd of people. A sign hung from the walking stick kept tempo. 'SHRIEKING GHOST TOURS!' the sign read, 'ARE YOU BRAVE ENOUGH?'

"She comes in the dead of night. A Murdered Mother seeking her Lost Child!" His voice raged in pitch. "Her Soul Rending

SHRIEKS tear up from the PITS!"

He jabbed his stick menacingly at the crowd, causing one young girl to screech. "Are you Brave Enough to come with me? Are you ready to SEE what can be SEEN at the SHRIEKING PITS?!"

I tried to sidestep his show, but he blocked my way. The mortician bent down and barked right into my face. His face was powdered white with teeth stained brown and breath that reeked of tobacco. "Well, are you? Do you think you are strong enough to face the horror of the Shrieking Woman of the Pit?"

I admit, I was taken aback by his confrontational speech and I stuttered a response, "Well, sir, I-"

"Don't let that ponce give you any trouble!" the hawker from the left side of the lane spoke up in my defense. He was dressed like a big game safari hunter, in browns and sandy khaki. On his head was a clean canvas Shikar helmet, just the sort of pith helmet I remember seeing punters, who had never seen actual fighting, wear in Afghanistan. Around his neck, he wore a sign, 'Fairy Hunts at The Shrieking Pits. TICKETS!'

"Shove off, Steven!" He swung a butterfly net at the mortician's head. "Come with me friend!" He took me by the arm and led me away. "Now, my friend, I can see you are a man of learning. Am I right, sir? I can see by the sharpness of your eye and the slant of your forehead that you are an educated man who needs something more material, something with an earthier quality to capture your imagination. Let me direct your attention to booth 13, right over there next to that yew tree. For the price of 10 pence, you can buy an adventure of a lifetime!" The impertinent cur grabbed my face, pinching my cheeks and turned me towards the tree.

"Hands off!" I said and pushed him away. I admit, my patience was wearing thin and it took some amount of control to only slap his hands away and not break them off at the wrist.

I worried that I would need to explain myself to his larger companion, but they merely shrugged and went off to find easier marks.

I took a deep breath and tried to gather my composure. This was a madhouse. A madhouse! How could these people have turned the tragedy of not just one but three missing people into a carnival? My head spun at the absolute callous nature of my fellow humans and my heart sank. Still, I had a job to do. I needed to find what passed for a police force in this out of the way village. As luck would have it, Mr. Donnelly saw me and came rushing over.

He laughed and planted a heavy hand on my shoulder. He wobbled a bit and I could smell beer on his breath. "Isn't it grand, Dr. Watson? Look around! The greenway hasn't seen such excitement since the last May Day Fair and that was held over ten, fifteen years ago, if memory serves me right. Oh, you should have seen them. Cor! Absolute wonders! People would come from miles around! Oh, and the women! Dancing and singing. And the beer! Oh, the times we had then, Dr. Watson. Back when the village was in its heyday."

"That's splendid but I need to ask you a question."

"Oh, I know you look around now and Almertune looks like some dingy, backwater village. A dirty cur that is barely crawling by on three legs, but we used to be something, back in the day. See this land here?" He stamped down with his boot, nearly toppling over. "Whoops! This land... this is a historical site, you know." He put his finger up to his mouth and made a sloppy, shushing noise. "Not many people knows about it. It's kept a secret."

"Why? If it could bring money into the village, why keep it a secret?"

"And let those dirty Royal shysters get a piece?" Mr. Donnelly's face flushed red. "Nobody outside the village has rights to it. Nobody! It's ours and no..." He burped, looked over my shoulder and the colour drained from his face. "Go... go and have a good time. Don't listen to me blathering. I think I need to find the facilities."

"Wait, you can help me. I need to find the constabulary. I want to talk to him about his investigation. I have some information I'd like to pass on."

Donnelly's eyes squinted. "Consta... constabulary? Oh... you mean old Dick Turner. He works over in Norwich. Almertune is too small for a proper police force so Constable Turner pops round when we need him. He was here a few days ago. Haven't seen him since. Figured he went back home. I'll send the boy to fetch him, if you'd like."

I sighed and tried to hold down my disappointment. "Yes, please. The sooner the better. If all turns out as I hope, we might have an answer to the mystery by nightfall."

"Oh, let's hope not quite so soon!" Mr. Donnelly put a finger to the side of his nose and stumbled away.

This news and the aloof nature of my host did nothing to help my mood. It was growing darker even as the sun rose higher in the sky. I continued through the crowds, hoping to find Mrs. Dowell or Mr. Todd when I spied the two young men from the train whom I'd thought were porters. Handsomely dressed wearing top hats and carrying smooth, black canes, I was obviously mistaken. They tipped their hats to me. "Good morning," they said in unison.

I returned their greeting with a bit of embarrassment. "Pardon my impertinence back on the train, sirs. I took you for porters."

They both smiled and exchanged a knowing look. Then one spoke, "Not to worry, Dr. Watson. Your trouble was reported to the authorities."

"All was taken care of. "

"Have a good day." And they both walked on, blending into the crowd.

A queer feeling swept over me. We met so briefly on the train that we barely had time for pleasantries. So how did they know my name?

I resolved to go after them when I saw the two thugs from the train, standing on the outskirts of the crowd. The taller one had his hand in a cast. The fat one had a black eye and a swollen lip. They were looking into the crowd, as if searching for someone. I had a cold feeling in my gut. I followed their line of sight and found Mrs. Dowell, fanning herself and frantically looking for Mr. Todd, completely unaware of the danger that lurked just out of bounds. I felt the heavy bump of my army pistol in my jacket pocket and pushed my way through the crowd.

"Excuse me!" I said through gritted teeth. "Pardon me! Please, make way!"

I stopped to get my bearings. I could see them, across the field but they might as well have been a continent away from the pace I was making. Mrs. Dowell was still on the move but completely unaware of the pair stalking her. I shouted her name but got no response. My voice simply melted in with the rest of the chaos. The thugs were getting closer and closer. Frustrated, I decided to throw social niceties to the wind and started running. I was closing in on Mrs. Dowell when...

"OOOF!"

I ran into something short and hard.

"ARRGH!What are ye doin'?!" The fellow cursed as we fell and rolled. I ended up on the top end and he pushed me over. "Get your carcass offin' me!" He lay there like a turtle, his arms flailing to his side. "Christ on a muffin, are ye jest gonna stan' there and gawk, man? Help a brokeback beggar back to his feet, will ye?"

I helped him up which was a harder job than I reckoned. His stature belied his weight. It was like pulling a horse out of ditch. He stood a foot shorter than me. A horrible hump on his back bent him over cruelly. "I am so sorry... I hope I didn't cause you any injury."

"None more than the Good Lord Himself saw fit to do to me already."

Standing erect, or as erect as the poor unfortunate could, I could see he was wearing an eye patch to cover a missing eye and had bruises on his face. He wore dirty, poor clothes cut a size too big for him to accommodate for the hump, I assumed.

"Howz about I take your photograph, Guv'nor? Only 5 pence. A sight better deal than that shyster with the poxy ponies," he said, as he hobbled over to a tripod that held dry plate camera.

"No... I'm quite busy..."

"Are ye now? Doing what, sir? If ye don't mine me askin', sir."

"Yes, I am with a friend... she needs me... I am trying to... oh, hang on." Across the way, I saw Mrs. Dowell and the two mysterious men from the train talking animatedly. She put her arms around one and kissed him, obviously happy to see him. There was more talking and the three walked away together, towards the woods and the Shrieking Pits; the thugs did not follow.

"Oh, maybe not."

"Oh, did yer lady friend find someone else? Shame. Can't be trusted, lady friends, I've always said. This is the only girl I can count on." He patted his camera. "She's never done me wrong. Brings me my bread and butter and never asks where I've been. Not like my Old Woman. Cor, what a nag. C'mon let me mend your broken heart. It's partially my fault you missed yor date, ain't it? Come on, let's get yer a photo... oh, damn!" he kicked at something on the ground. "It's fallen over. I have a horrible time, getting it upright, with me back and all. Could ye do the honors, sir? Least ye can do... since it is partially, if you don't mind me pointing out, sir, yer fault that it is in the mud and all."

"Fine," I sighed. This strange little man was becoming more of a burden than I needed in my life right now. I reached down and pulled off the ground a life sized wooden cut out of...

"Oh my word..."

"Do ye like him? I carved it up myself. I coulda done a better job if'n I'd the time and proper tools and such but, it does the job, doncha' think, sir? A proper likeness of him, if I do say so meself."

It was a stand up cut out of Sherlock Holmes or I should say, a stand up cut out of one of Mr. Paget's more famous drawings that portrayed Holmes in my stories, as published in the Strand. It was perfect, right down to the deerstalker hat, which Holmes had never actually worn. The only thing missing was a face. Where that should have been, there was only a hole.

"Where is his face?"

"Ah, that's the beauty of the gimmick, sir. Ye put yer mug right in here," he stood behind it and stretched to fit his face in the hole, "and for the price of a few pennies, the punters, excusing yerself, sir, get a chance to stand in for The Great Detective! Ye know of him, sir?"

"Yes, as a matter of fact, I..."

"Oh! I thought I could spot a fellow admirer! Yer an enthusiast, ain't you, sir?"

"An enthusiast?"

"Of the stories! Of The Great Detective, Sherlock Holmes! Oh, we can't get enough. My wife and me, we buys every edition of the Strand whens we see that the good Doctor has written up another tale. Such ripping yarns, doncha think? My favorite was the one with the ghost dog. Cor! Gave me the night terrors. But I

never did like curs before and certainly not since reading that tale, I can tell ye."

"Sir, I am confused. You do realize that they aren't fiction, don't you? They really happened."

"What? All that stuff they print in the Strand?"

"Yes, they did."

"With the pictures and the drawings? Cor! No!"

"Yes! I should know. I..."

"No! Yer having a laugh at me now, sir." The little man pushed me away and laughed. "Git off! Real? Everybody knows they ain't real. Oh, sure, them big city editors at The Strand makes out like they are the 'true adventures of Sherlock Holmes', but everybody knows," he put a dirty finger up to the side of his nose and tapped it, winking at me. "everybody knows, he ain't real."

"But he is!"

"Naw... he's not."

"Yes!"

"A figgerment of your imagination, I think." The hunchback snorted a laugh. "Don't try to pull one over on me. I knows a tale when I hears it."

"No sir!" I toppled the wooden figure down to the ground and stomped on it with my boot. My anger had finally boiled over and the receptacle for it was the unfortunate specimen in front of me. "No, sir! I will not stand for it! Sherlock Holmes is real! All those adventures I wrote truly happened, sir! I know because I lived them, side by side, with my friend, Sherlock Holmes. For you to stand there and tell me any different is to call me a liar!"

The little man grinned and held up his hands. "All right, all right, Calm down..."

But there was no calming down, I had more venom to spew and I could no more hold in the bile than could a drunkard hold back his vomit. "Furthermore, I find it horribly offensive that this village is using the disappearances and, very probably, the deaths of three innocent people, one of them my dear friend, as an excuse to throw a blasted carnival! It is disgusting, inhumane and definitely not English!"

"Please, my dear Watson, you are attracting attention..."

"I came down here to find my friend, thinking the worst and finding that no one else in this whole blasted village seems to even give a damn... wait, what did you call me?"

The little hunchback lifted up the eye patch and winked at me with a shining, gray eye.

"Holmes!"

"Hello, Watson, it is good to see you, too. I do hope that you had the foresight to bring some clean clothes for me. Some scoundrel stole my luggage!"

CHAPTER NINE

OAKENCREST'S MOUNT

Holmes instructed me to wait a half hour before following him to the cottage where he was staying. He gave me directions to a location in the woody outskirts of the village, close to the Pits but far enough away to be avoided by the festivalgoers. I followed his directions to the letter but, blast! I soon became lost. The woods were thick with brush, birds and flora. The day had grown humid and gnats pestered me like a plague. I ached for something cold to drink. Soon every tree began to look the same. The sky was beginning to become dark with storm clouds and I could feel the air getting ripe for another storm. I began to despair and started to backtrack my footsteps in hopes that I would at least find my way back to the festival when I heard a shrill whistle come from behind me. It sent shivers up my spine. I turned to see a door made entirely from earth open up in front of me. Holmes waved me inside the earthen cottage.

"Ingenious, isn't it? Shades of Dartmoor, don't you think?" he said, reminding me of the cabin he stayed in during our adventure with the Hound. He closed the door behind me and locked it with a simple wooden latch. Inside, it was cozy although a tad Spartan for my taste; with only a table, chairs and two wooden platforms set above the floor that doubled as either a couch or bed for furnishings. While my military leanings like a neat and tidy place, the furnishing here was damn near medieval. As my eyes adjusted to the dim light provided by the oil lamps, I noticed a man lying on the bed. He nodded at me and I returned the greeting, even as I shuddered from the sudden drop in temperature, however slight.

"The entire cottage is integrated into the hillside behind it. There is wattle and daub insulation between the oak planks, an open hearth with a concealed smokestack. Oh but don't be fooled. There is a warren of other rooms further back and some that have doors that lead outside." Holmes barely took a breath as he continued pontificating about his hidey hole while lighting another lamp. "This has been in his family for generations, Watson. The surrounding earth has completely overtaken it, like a green blanket. It is absolutely perfect camouflage! I tell you, Watson, we have so much to learn from those who came before us!"

I sat down hard on the wooden pallet from exhaustion. My heart was spent. "Good Lord, Holmes! Don't you know that all of England has been looking for you? Is this where you've been hiding?"

"It wasn't from England that I was hiding, my good man." He unbuckled his vest, slipped out of his mud-soaked blouse and slowly, painfully, pulled a knapsack over his head and dropped it on the floor with a loud thud. He groaned as he stood to his full height, stretching and pulling his arms and back into place. "My word, Watson, you have no idea the agony of a tall man pretending not to be. Oh, here!" He reached inside his tunic, pulled out a package wrapped in a checkered napkin, and threw it towards the man on the cot. "Before I forget, here's a nice hunk of chicken breast. Sorry if it is a bit crushed. Had a run in with an old friend."

The man caught the bundle and smiled greedily. "Ta, mate!"

"Holmes! Did you steal that chicken?"

"I prefer the term 'appropriated', Watson. One does as one needs to avoid starvation. Speaking of which, you must be thirsty. There is an icebox next to my pallet. I think I have a few beers left."

I found the box and took out a brown, cold bottle of beer. I eagerly drank it and felt instantly refreshed. "Thanks! That is exactly what I needed."

"They have an excellent brew master nearby." He poured some water into a bowl and washed his face, toweling off, gingerly. He turned to face me and I could see deep purple bruising on his face. "I really must see if I can get him some business when I get back to London."

"Good Lord, man! What happened to you?" I went to see if I could render aid.

"What? This?" His thin, pale hands made circular motions in the air, waving me away. "It's nothing. One of the hazards of being the rescuer of that bag."

I kicked the bag. Something very hard and jingly inside made me regret the action instantly. "Are you going to tell me or make me guess?"

Holmes sat down next to me, crossed his legs and prepared his pipe. His shirt now hung on him like a dirty, stained choir robe. He smelled twice as bad. He wiggled his eyebrows as he took his first drag. "You've come this far down the rabbit hole, I'm sure you must have some idea by now."

I nodded, pulled the coin out of my pocket and held it up with a sense of glee.

He clapped his slender hands and laughed. "Ah! So Mycroft sent you! Excellent! That is good news. Soon, I'll be back in Baker Street and a hot bath!"

"No, no... I haven't spoken to your brother. I found this coin in your luggage."

"My luggage? How did you come by it? It was... oh! Oh...

no." Holmes' face sank. His teeth ground into his pipe stem. "Todd. Damn that blasted man! How did you come to meet him?"

"I had just returned to London when my housekeeper shoved the paper in my face, full of stories of your disappearance. I barely had time to register what had happened when she then informed me that Mr. Todd and Mrs. Dowell were waiting for me

in my study. They told me you had come down here to look for a vanished couple that Todd was utterly convinced was abducted..."

"By fairies." He puffed his pipe in irritation. "Yes, I spent a very long train ride being tutored on the criminal dealings of the fairy underworld. But surely you know me better than that, Watson? Why would you even entertain such a ludicrous thought that I would spend precious time to go fairy hunting?"

"No, I thought..."

"Did it ever occur to you to contact my brother?"

"I didn't have time! I..."

"Or Inspector Lestrade? Admittedly, he isn't the sharpest knife in the dull drawer that is Scotland Yard, but still! No, you just go bounding off with a madman and his deadly nursemaid! Astounding! It begs the question, Watson, exactly how stupid did your sabbatical make you?"

"I never believed you were abducted by fairies, Holmes!" All the fire I feared I had lost came raging back as I stood up and shouted, "I assumed that you had slipped back into your old habits!"

"Ah." He slid away from me, pulled up his knees and leaned against the wall. He looked at me over his kneecaps, his gray eyes watering from the pipe smoke. "Is that what you think of me, Watson? A mental cripple? A degenerate? Some poor devil that, without your constant companionship, would fling himself headfirst into a drug induced delirium? That I'd follow some madman to the ends of the earth; leave my home and hearth to run screaming, into this vile backwoods, searching for figments of his twisted imagination? Ha! Why am I surprised? I should have deduced as much from the twaddle you write. Your pen reveals your true feelings, I fear." He clapped his hands and steepled his fingers under his chin. His eyes were gleaming as he stared down over them at me. "So, enlighten me, *Doctor*." I felt a tightening in my throat, the same sort a rabbit must have in the grips of a snake. "I assume that, in the beginning of your latest solo adventure, you and your new friends went to my apartment in Baker Street?"

"Yes."

"And Mrs. Hudson just let you barge into my private rooms?"

"Well, yes, she did."

"Hrmph. I must have words with her."

"I did use the secret key you told me about."

"Hmrph. Then that part is on me," Holmes grumbled. "Still! You must have seen my work! The photographs, the maps, the twine that I had linking them all to the Pit, the books. There was even a letter from Mycroft himself! You had all the clues staring you directly in the face, if you could only read them."

"I saw them! The shipping maps and the timetables. The books on Vikings and fairies. I damn well stabbed myself in the rear with your damn tin fairy!"

He seemed delighted at the image of his tin fairy jabbing me in the backside and smiled if only briefly. "Then, tell me, Doctor, what slippery steppingstones did you find that led you to the conclusion that I was in the grips of a drug induced delirium?"

"Your needle!" I pointed excitedly at him "Aha! It was missing from its case! Explain that!"

Holmes pinched the bridge of his nose and inhaled deeply. "Did you check the wastepaper bin?"

"What?"

"It was broken. I put it in the bin beside my desk."

"Oh."

"Isn't that rich, Steven? Oh, where are my manners? Dr. John Watson let me introduce my erstwhile companion in this adventure and our host, Steven Oakencrest. Steven, this is the man I've spoken so much about to you. My *friend*," his teeth snapped as he said the words, "Dr. John Watson."

"'ullo." The man on the wooden pallet bed sat up, groaning at the exertion. He was missing an eye and his face was even more bruised than Holmes. As he turned towards me, his remarkable silhouette made me gasp.

"Another hunchback?"

"The original, actually." Holmes tossed him the eyepatch. Steven nodded thanks and slipped it on. "I needed a new identity so I could keep watch and Steven gratefully loaned me his. Why else would I dress like this? Couldn't have a one-eyed hunchback suddenly show up in the middle of the village green. People would talk."

"Who beat him so?"

Holmes pointed towards the saddlebag. "Mutual acquaintances who want that bag. Or, to be precise, what is in that bag."

Pieces of the puzzle began to snap together in my mind. "The treasure! The one the thugs wanted from us on the train!"

"Thugs?"

"Yes, they attacked me and then went after Mr. Todd. They kept screaming at him, 'where's the treasure, where did he take it?' It was then that I knew that this went deeper than your addiction."

"I do *not* have an *addiction*!"

I took a deep breath and kept my voice calm. "I meant that I started this because I was deeply concerned about your well-being. I am your friend and your doctor. Your health is paramount to me, if not, from what I can gather from your lifestyle, very much, to you."

His teeth clenched on the pipe stem. He puffed out a cloud of smoke in irritation. "That isn't important. These thugs, the ones you encountered on the train, Watson, tell me everything. You know my methods. Don't leave anything out, no matter how inconsequential it may seem to you."

I proceeded to tell him of what had transpired in the past 18 hours. I was amazed when I realized that it not even a day had passed since I started on this quest; it felt more like a week.

I told him about the train ride and Todd's drugged stupor. I heard Holmes cough and mutter, "Addict." I ignored this jibe and told him of Mrs. Dowell's agitation and her concerns regarding Mr. Todd.

I omitted the invitation for drinks for propriety's sake.

"Then, two men burst into our car. They assaulted me first, then threatened Mrs. Dowell and then attacked the sleeping Mr. Todd, asking over and over again for the treasure. Due to my injuries, I was unable to retaliate but, as it turned out, I didn't need to! Mrs. Dowell in two or three moves broke one man's arm and knocked the other man unconscious!"

Holmes smiled. "From what I know of Mrs. Dowell, I am not surprised. She is a quite an indomitable force of womanhood. Describe the two men to me, no... let me guess. One was tall, with a sharp, weasely face and the other was squat, dangerously handy with a very wicked shillelagh."

"The very ones."

Holmes nodded at the man on the pallet and grunted.

"Aye," Steven grunted. "I know that stick."

"We both do, my friend." He rubbed his swollen jaw. "The short man is McKenzie Potts. A blacksmith by trade, obvious if you had the presence of mind to take notice the keloid scars on his hands. The tall man is a small-time thief, Robbie Tyrone. He has spent a few turns in Millbank. Neither of them is the brains of this operation." Holmes' thin fingers did a circular dismissive wave. "Obviously. No. That person is still unknown to me."

"Both Potts and Tyrone are here. I saw them both at the festival. They were hiding on the edges, stalking Mrs. Dowell. I intended to warn her but that is when I, quite literally, ran into you."

"Oh? Was she the woman friend you spoke of?" A sly grin slid across his lips. "I am very sorry for the intrusion, dear fellow."

"Luckily, as it turned out, she didn't need me. The two men I had assumed were train porters approached her and, from the way she reacted, she knew them. One of them, it seems from the way she greeted him, she knew very well."

"Watson, jealousy doesn't become you." Holmes rolled his eyes at my bitter disappointment. "Wait. What did you mean, 'assumed to be porters'?"

"After the two thugs ran out of our car, I went after them and found two men standing in the corridor. From their dark suits, I assumed they were porters, so I told them what happened. Earlier today, I saw them again at the festival. From their manners and, quite frankly, expensive clothing, I concluded they were definitely not porters."

Holmes nodded, his eyes drew into slits. "Were they

impeccably dressed? Walked almost in unison? They both had clipped Oxford speech?"

I nodded.

Holmes leaned back against the wall and laughed. "Mycroft! Excellent! I'd hoped he would send someone when I hadn't contacted him. This is all falling into place. If the thieves stay on schedule, they will be attempting to get the next shipment to the dock by tomorrow. Surely, you heard about the Shrieking Whatsit being spotted?"

"Yes, to the West, far off its normal track."

"To set the erstwhile investigators on the wrong track. They are thieves by trade, Watson, not murderers. There has been enough bloodshed already."

"The lunching couple?"

"Christopher Benson and his lady friend. Yes. I am afraid so."

"Why didn't Constable Turner find their corpses?"

"Who?" Holmes arched an eyebrow as he bit down on his pipe. "I have no knowledge of the man. He's either been bought off, as many of these small-town constables are so ready to be, or dead. I haven't been able to venture back to the Pits, unfortunately. It's a shame, either way, but don't worry, old chum, it will all come out right in the end. The Diogenes boys can catch them in the act and all will be settled. Bravo! My brother's timing is always superb."

"Oh, yes!" I exclaimed, reaching into my pocket. "I'd almost forgotten. I have a telegraph from him."

"You do?"

"It's for you. It was delivered after you..."

"Were taken off by the Fairy King?"

"Yes." I gave him a blank sheet of paper. "It's written in lemon juice."

"I can smell." Holmes took the glass chimney off the lamp and held the paper above the flame. The letters blossomed like magic on the page. "An old boyhood pastime of ours. Sending secret notes to one another. Dear Mycroft does love the classics."

He read the message and made a whistling noise between his teeth. "Ah, well. Sorry old boy. A little too late for that I fear." He dipped a corner of the paper in the fire until it caught and tossed the flaming paper onto the floor. He turned to me, a triumphant smile on his face. "Still, now that we have help on our doorstep courtesy of the Diogenes Club, all our worries will soon be put to rest! By the way, where did you see them last?"

"With Mrs. Dowell. I believe they were going into the woods, towards the Shrieking Pits."

Holmes' smiled faded and his gray eyes locked with mine. "For heaven's sake, why?"

"To search for Mr. Todd, I presume. He was very determined to use his new gadget that he received from America."

"The electrospectrascope transponder? He told me something of it. I don't remember much, I started to blank him out after an hour or so. I remember something about a tinkerer in America, who was putting one together for him. He thought he could bridge communications between the spheres or some such rot."

"He was going to use it to contact the fairies and bargain for your release. When I showed him the telegram from Mycroft and then told him that I suspected you came here for duplicitous reasons, it made him very upset. He was more determined than ever."

"Duplicitous? Why would you say that, Watson? You might as well have spit in his face. Now he feels used, abandoned and humiliated."

"I'm sorry, Holmes, but he is an adult and needed to know the truth!"

"Ulysses K. Todd is a delusional young man with enough money to keep him cocooned inside his fantasy world. Surely, in all of your *conversations* with Mrs. Dowell, she must have made that much clear."

"The damned fool will get himself kilt, that's for sure," Steven groaned. "He's headed toward the mouth of the monster, that he is."

"At minimum, he'll only get himself killed." Holmes paced quickly across the dirt floor, staring down with his chin on his chest. He shook his head in quick bursts, as if rejecting thoughts and pushing them out of his head. Finally, he stopped and gave a shout. "Blast! There is no other recourse. We have to go after them. Damn! I was so close to a hot bath and a proper cup of coffee. No offense, my dear Steven, but I am and will always be a city mouse at heart. Blast it all to hell! I only hope we find them before more blood is shed!"

"Should I come with ye?" Steven asked. "You might need another set of fists."

"No. I thank you for the offer, but you are still too injured." Holmes picked up the saddlebag and swung it over his shoulder. "Come, Watson! You have your revolver, I trust?"

I patted my jacket. "Yes. As always, it is at your service."

"Capital, Watson. I'll explain as we go and fill in the gaps as quickly as I can. Let us go and pray we aren't too late!"

CHAPTER TEN

'ONE WILL FIND THE OTHER.'

"Do you see them, Watson? No? Well, don't berate yourself. I'm ashamed to confess that I completely passed them by at first as well. Oh! What treasures we'd discover if we'd only take the time to look and see the mysteries that surround us!"

Holmes was walking at a brisk pace in front of me, passionately pointing out what looked to me to be small grass covered mounds, like humps in a field. He climbed on top of one and stamped down his foot. His gray eyes sparkled with that look which, I knew too well, came when he was infatuated with a new idea. "Amazing! It really is quite remarkable, the architectural marvels of the ancients. To be able to accomplish such wonders with so little. Well, what we modern folk would consider impoverished conditions, anyway."

I did a double step to catch up with him and confessed, red faced, "You have me completely stumped, Holmes. What am I looking at?"

"If you'd taken the time to read one of the historical reference books I had back at my flat, instead of jumping to conclusions," Holmes said, as he jumped nimbly down from the mound, the heavy saddlebag of silver coins over his shoulder causing him no problem at all, "you'd be better informed."

"Holmes... please, just tell me."

"Vikings, Watson! Surely, you knew that Vikings settled in these parts centuries ago. These few mounds are what are left of their humble homestead. These few have been completely consumed by the earth. Only the shelter used by the Oakencrests as a hunting blind remains usable. Oh, can you imagine what we might find if we dug out these mounds? And the Shrieking Pits? Ha! Those circular pits all the spiritualists and dunderheads are so giddy over are merely the remains of the foundations of *these* archaeological treasure troves. As are what I carry over my shoulder." He patted the bags reverently. "I see you are still confused. Come, Watson, keep up and I'll start from the beginning."

He started walking eastward, his long legs taking two strides as compared to my one. I won't lie; it had been a long time since I'd had to march double-time and I struggled to keep alongside him as he spoke.

"You were correct about one thing, I will admit. The weeks after your departure were very hard and I was tempted, many times. There was very little to keep the roaring engine that is my mind on track. Oh, yes, there were tidbits in the news to occupy me for a moment or two. The Shopshire Chopper was at it again, much to the terror of little old ladies and their cats. There was an interesting article in the Lancet regarding experimentation on the coagulation of blood platelets that I was able to completely refute in my own little kitchen laboratory. Oh! And to add to my hellish misery, Mrs. Hudson somehow found herself under the delusion that she has an ear for music. She began voice lessons with someone at her church and is constantly singing, singing, singing! It was hell, Watson, as if someone was running a sharp fork up and down my spine. Torture, sheer aural torture! Just as I was about to reach my breaking point, I received a telegram from my brother. As I have said, his timing is preternatural. He wanted me to meet with him at the Diogenes Club to discuss a problem he felt was more befitting my line of work. Or, as he so often defines it, 'leg work'. Do you know, Watson, it saddens me to think of the heights my brother could attain if only his morbid laziness did not confine him to the corridors of Whitehall or his blasted Club!

"I met with him the next day and over a lunch of squab he told me of his quandary. There were unusual shipments of silver coming out of a port in Norfolk every three weeks on the dot. Which caught his eye since Norfolk is noted for linen and textiles, not minerals. He asked if I would look into it. As you saw, by the maps and books back at Baker Street, I looked into the problem without hesitation. I believe I went through two pounds of shag tobacco ruminating."

"I believe that. The room was still rank with the smell when I visited the other day."

"It is a heavy tobacco, for sure. The oily smoke leaves a very crispy ash..." Holmes shook his head as if trying to shake away the divergent line of thought. "Anyway, with the help of my confederate, Steven Oakencrest, and his own brand of 'legwork' I was able to piece the puzzle together in the matter of a few days. Someone had found a hidden trove of Viking silver. Not that unusual, really. It was just over fifty years ago that they found that hoard of silver in Lancashire, remember? No? Well, someone has found another sizable hoard and, instead of informing the British Government, who would have legal ownership and would seize it for the Royal treasury, was smelting it down into bars and smuggling it out to a buyer. Amazingly simple, really. I worry if my brother is ill?"

"Ah, I see," I said although I was still quite in the dark. "And how do the fairies play into it?"

"Fairies?" Holmes stopped so abruptly I nearly ran into him. "There are no fairies! Good Lord, man, have you hit your head?"

"But then why involve Ulysses Todd in this?"

"I needed a cover, obviously. I couldn't just come down here, The Great Detective, and have a look, could I? Thanks to you, my reputation is known everywhere! It would let the villains know I was on to them and they would have bolted like rabbits. Also, it became personal when I found what they had done to my friend, Steven, in the course of his duty to me. It was natural to use the cover of helping the erratic and eccentric Ulysses K. Todd to investigate the Supernatural Kidnapping of the Lunching Couple. Oh, yes—that is the title he was planning on using for his treatise. Our friend, Ulysses, has literary aspirations, the same, as I believe you do, Watson. Yet, I'd be actually using my time to find the cache of Viking silver and retrieve it. Or that, at least, was my thinking... up to a point."

"Up to a point?"

He shifted the saddlebags on his shoulder and coughed nervously. "Things became... complicated."

I said nothing. Holmes walked on in silence, his eyes downward, considering his words carefully. Even his gait slowed down. I knew my friend well and, when he fell into moods like this, it was best to remain quiet until he was ready to continue. Therefore, I remained silent, his steadfast companion.

"Perhaps, I am becoming too slow, Watson. Age, it comes to us all. These vessels of flesh in which we are forced to live, inevitably break down and rot. There is no escaping. Sometimes, I fear I am getting too old for this game."

I waited a beat, knowing he wanted no empty words of consolation. In fact, such a display would repulse him. After the beat passed, I asked, simply. "What happened?"

"I'm sure Todd told you of the coin he found?"

"Yes. He was quite ecstatic. He thought it was fairy money."

Holmes smiled and laughed heartily. "I envy that man's simple-mindedness. Really, I do. It must be so refreshingly easy." He took a deep breath, shifted the load on his shoulder and trudged forward at his normal pace. That is to say, twice mine.

"SO, I was confident that I had found at least somewhere near their base of operations. While Todd and Dowell meandered around the pits with their pendulums and other occult gadgets, I looked further afield for something more suitable for a blacksmith. I couldn't see any but, luckily, my other senses kept me on track."

"Oh?"

He tapped the side of his sizable nose. "The olfactory sense is such an underappreciated one, Watson. I could smell a distinct taint of sulphur in the air. I knew there was smelting being done somewhere nearby. After Todd found the coin, I suggested we go back into town to celebrate. This was a ruse, of course. I had planned to first go alone back to the Pits, so I could search in privacy, and then meet up with them at the restaurant. However, as I said, things became complicated."

"Am I to assume the complications are the origins of your bruises?"

A quick smile flitted across his face. "Yes, as well as others you have yet to see. I was not alone. Damn it, Watson! How could I not have noticed? He came up on me like a shadow! I was as blind and deaf as..."

"Anyone else? My dear Holmes, as much as I admire you, you are only human, you know."

"That is becoming more and more apparent to me," he said, grimacing. "I found the mound they were using as a blacksmith shop. The space is much like Steven's, except the airshaft on top has been fitted and adapted. Oh, the smells, Watson! And the sounds! I understand now where the legend of the Shrieking Pit got its start. Metal screams when as it melts, Watson, did you know that? It is a horrible sound. Poured into the molds, it shrieks and spits as it cools into a new form. Wagner was right to cast it into an opera. And the smells, Watson. Overpowering to an instrument as sensitive as mine."

"Holmes," I said firmly. I could see he was procrastinating. His train of thought would meander around things he didn't want to think on. "What happened?"

He stopped and took a deep breath. I could see the tension in his jaw muscles as he clenched his teeth. "Bah! I was caught, Watson, like a novice I was so entranced by the flame, Watson. The next thing I knew..." He waved at the bruises on his face. "Robbie Tyrone. Outside the mound. With Pott's shillelagh. He beat me mercilessly. I'm amazed I only lost one tooth. I woke up, on the floor inside the mound, my hands and feet trussed like a pig. I overheard them arguing about the couple they'd had to kill, because they had unknowingly stumbled upon their operations while looking for a secluded place to... well, couple. Unlike those two poor innocents, I had a reputation, thanks to you again, Watson, and they argued as to whether or not to kill me. To settle their argument, they left to consult with the Boss, obviously the brains of the operation, whoever that may be. After they were gone, I freed myself. You know that I make a hobby of knots and escapology. There is a new magician just starting to make his name in America who is quite the expert at locks and escaping from straightjackets, I am told."

"Holmes..."

He sighed. "I scooped as many of the coins as I could fit into a saddlebag and ran back to the Oakencrest mound. The next afternoon, I ventured back to the hotel, but found that Todd and Dowell had left. And, even more vexing, my luggage was missing."

"Just as all of England believed you were."

"Yes. That is where it everything became so very... complicated. Not just for me, but for our erstwhile smugglers as well. I don't think they are counting on the greed of the village elders to concoct a circus to cash in on my unfortunate disappearance. It's really caused a cramp in their lives as much as mine. Ah, we are here."

I was so engrossed in Holmes' tale, I had not noticed how far we had walked into the woods. All around us the canopy of the trees was thick with greenery. Birds fluttered above and I could see the scampering of some ground vermin. The freshness from

the morning shower had boiled away in the sun and left in its place, air that was muggy with humidity. I pulled at my shirt collar for relief. The clouds above were beginning to turn a mottled sort of gray that promised another rainstorm in an hour or so. Footprints from the festivalgoers flattened the ground and trailed all around but, for the moment, we were the only visitors.

Ahead of us, the Shrieking Pits—three deep indentations ranging from 6 to 10 feet in radius, arranged in a V shape. It was an astounding sight, so incongruous with the surrounding woodland. I walked towards the center one and the air felt suddenly cooler and silent, as though the birdsong could not penetrate. I remarked that the mouth of each pit was a strange, darker shade of green than the surrounding lawn. Holmes' began to pontificate about the decomposition of old wood or mineral deposits being responsible for the colorations, but I paid scarce attention to his lecturing. There was something wrong here. My hackles were up. Intuitions that had kept me alive during my days in Afghanistan were prickling. I would never bring such things up to Holmes, he would only wave it away as more evidence of my romantic, dreamy nature but... there was something wrong here. My hand went to my pocket and I felt comforted by the cold metal of my gun.

"Well, halloa!" Holmes squatted. "Watson, come and see."

I hastened to his side. Laying in the grass, was Todd's electrospectrascope box, smashed to bits, tubes and wiring poured out of its casing like intestines. "My word, Holmes. This does not bode well."

"So, this is Todd's precious transponder box? Yes? That is bad. So, now comes the question," Holmes stood up and wiped his hands on his trousers, "what became of Mr. Todd?"

"That is exactly what I'd like to ask you, Mr. Holmes."

I turned around to see Mrs. Dowell step out from behind a tree, holding a pistol straight at us. From her earlier display, I took it for granted that she was also a deadly shot. The two men Holmes believed were Diogenes agents followed immediately behind her.

"Ah, I was wondering where you were all hiding," Holmes said, smiling as he held his hands aloft. "Good evening, gentlemen. Did you have trouble finding her?"

"We weren't sent to follow Bernadine. Our reunion was merely a happy coincidence, Mr. Holmes." The agent on the right stepped forward. He stood a head taller than I, and had that smarmy look I associated with the gambling type. He took the gun from Mrs. Dowell's hand. I was amazed that she resisted only slightly. "Thank you, dear, there's no reason for that, is there? Permit me to introduce myself. I am Agent Blake Featherstone. That man there is Agent Thomas Gordon. We were sent to find you."

"Oh, well. Congratulations."

"Thank you. I appreciate it, I really do. Frankly, it was a wild shot in the dark. You see, Mr. Holmes, your brother was rather cryptic in his directions in finding you."

"Oh? Do enlighten me."

"He said to follow Dr. John Watson. His exact words were, 'One will find the other.' And, what do you know? He was right!"

"And I am glad to see you, truly." Holmes walked over to the agents and handed them the saddlebags. "I have a good portion of the silver hoard in this saddlebag. It is not the full cache, but it is all I could liberate. The smugglers have probably melted down the rest into bars. If things go according to schedule, they should be moving the last of whatever they've smelted out to the docks tonight. If you would follow me."

"Wait!" Mrs. Dowell protested. "Have you forgotten someone? Ulysses! Where is he? Something horrible has happened to him, I know it. Just look at the box! He would never give up his electrospectrascope! He's my responsibility, Mr. Holmes."

"Yes, he is, Mrs. Dowell, so I suggest that you be off with it." Holmes waved her away. "Gentlemen, if you'd follow me, the base of operations is right over that ridge."

"You brute!" Mrs. Dowell snarled as she lunged at Sherlock Holmes. She grabbed him by his shoulders and with the ease of a tigress flipped him onto his back and pinned him with a knee against his neck. She snapped her head towards the three of us standing back and flashed a cold as steel look that let us know it was best not to interfere.

"He *trusted* you. It was only because of you and all those letters you sent him, praising him, stroking up his confidence, that set him off on this hellish adventure! When he thought they had taken you, it nearly killed him. It was one more millstone around his neck. Another victim he believed he fed to the fairies!"

Holmes croaked, "What?"

"Oh, dear me. Could there be something the brilliant Mr. Sherlock Bloody Holmes doesn't know? Let me fill in some gaps for you, Mr. Great Detective. When Ulysses was three years old, his mother took him to the river even though he was afraid of the water. As you can imagine, a lonely boy with a crooked spine and twisted foot was not much of a swimmer. But, his dear Mother told him fairies lived there and they would be his friends.

"That's how she got him to go into the river, Mr. Holmes. With the promise of friends.

"You see, dear Mother was tired of taking care of a crippled boy she never wanted in the first place. The doctors all said he would die in the first year, but the boy continued to stubbornly stay alive. So, she decided to take fate into her own hands. She held his little head under water, thinking he would die, but he fought back. The terrible woman slipped and fell into the river. They never found her body. Ulysses was found three days later, a crippled, traumatized little boy whose mind concocted the story of water fairies that took his mother away from him, but left him behind because he wasn't *perfect*." Mrs. Dowell spit the word out like poison. "Do you see why he wants so much to communicate with the fairies? He thinks he can get his mother back. That little boy still, after all these years, just wants his mother. That is who you used, who you tricked with your oh-so-clever words and schemes. A scared, grieving, boy! So, remember that when you are safely back at Baker Street, smoking your foul pipe and sitting on your God-forsaken laurels!"

Mrs. Dowell slapped Holmes across the face before taking her knee of his neck. She stood over him as he looked up at her, his eyes wide, in what emotion, I couldn't fathom to guess. He slowly sat up and said, very somberly, "I had no idea. Truly, I am ashamed. What do you want me to do?"

"Help me to find him," she brushed a tear with the palm of her hand, "before the silly fool gets himself killed."

Holmes stood up and brushed himself off. He walked over to Mrs. Dowell, took her hand and gently held it as he spoke. "I swear to you, I will do all in my humble power to find him. And, although my past actions do not reflect it, I assure you, my word is my bond."

She grasped his hands in a firm handshake. Her sparkling hazel eyes drilled into his stern gray ones. "Then prove it."

CHAPTER ELEVEN

THE CHALLENGE ACCEPTED

Thomas Gordon and Blake Featherton, the agents sent by Mycroft Holmes, both suggested that we retrace our steps, starting back at the hotel, but Holmes quickly pish-poshed their ideas. "Why go back to the starting point when we have all we need right here, where the mystery began?"

"Let's begin with the box. It is smashed in by something heavy. A foot? No. There is no evidence of mud or boot prints." He rubbed his jaw. "I can't think of many things heavy enough to break through a box as sturdy as that."

He started following a trail. "See? These footprints here? This is where we start."

"There are lots of footprints, all around," Agent Gordon said. "Why those?"

"Because our Mr. Todd has a club foot. See the slight dragging mark?" Holmes mimicked Todd's unusual gait. "You won't see that sort of mark on a ballet dancer. Only someone like Todd. Come. There are two other prints ahead. He was chasing them. Yes, see here! There was a scuffle between the three men. One was Todd, definitely. Another was a taller man, slight of build... you can tell by the width apart of the prints and the depth they made in the mud. The other pair... oh, no... a shorter man, stockier. I fear I know that man. Yes. A fight happened here. See? Drops of blood there and over there."

"Oh no!" Mrs. Dowell murmured.

"Do not mourn yet! The slim man ran in that direction." Holmes pointed to the West, back towards the festival ground. "The stockier man went in that direction." He looked towards the East and grimaced. He followed the tracks for a few feet. "He was dragging something. I fear it was our friend. I fear I know where this leads. Still, there is hope! I do not believe our stocky friend would bother dragging a corpse. Come! We follow the tracks. Hurry now! The sky is growing angrier and I have no desire to be caught in a storm!"

We men scampered to keep up with him. When Sherlock Holmes finds a scent, he is like a greyhound, a force of lean muscle and tenacity. He would stop for a bit, pick up a twig, twist a bit of grass between his finger and then back to the trail! This sudden burst of energy and athleticism was no surprise to me, but I could tell by the red faces and sweating of the two young Diogenes agents, that they felt more than a bit challenged

The only one who seemed unimpressed with Holmes' physical display was Mrs. Dowell who matched him, stride for stride.

It was easily understandable. She was the one who had the most invested. This is what I believed moved her forward with such strength and determination. Her duty to Ulysses K. Todd went further than just his personal secretary and nurse. I believe she held a sisterly devotion to the fragile, broken man. She wanted to shield him, protect him, even if it was from himself. Watching her, tirelessly and fearlessly charging through God only knew what, to defend someone she steadfastly declared was "not a relationship", made my fondness for her grow a thousand-fold. She was, indeed, as Holmes declared, an indomitable force of womanhood.

Holmes held up a thin pale hand and we all stopped. "The earth here has been moved. Watson, what do you observe?"

I stepped up beside my friend and looked down on the ground. "Graves, I would say. Shallow ones. Three. Those two there on the left are older, the dirt has had time to settle because of the rains. The third one is fresher."

"Exactly what I deduced. Those two," his fingers pointed at the two on the left, "are the resting places of the lunching couple. This one on the right, I do not have enough evidence to hazard a guess."

"No!" Mrs. Dowell began tearing at the ground with her hands.

Holmes nodded towards the agents who also began to help her dig. They very soon discovered a burlap bag entwined in a thin rope. Agent Featherton opened a pocketknife and sliced through the fabric. A foul gas of decomposition erupted from the grave, causing us all to take a step back.

"Who is it? Who is it?" Mrs. Dowell asked.

"Not Todd," Holmes replied. "The face is not familiar to me. Do any of you know him? No? Perhaps he is the Constable you mentioned, Watson?"

I shrugged and took a shallow breath. "I have no idea, Holmes."

"Pity. Yet, still hope remains! I suspect that Todd must have somehow crossed paths with our smugglers. The mound they work out of is just around that bend. I only hope he has the same luck with them that I did."

It was still early in the evening, but the dark clouds gathering overhead made it seem nearer to dusk. Holmes put a finger to his lips, motioning us to be quiet as we moved towards the mound.

As we drew closer, the air was pungent, a smell worse than that which we uncovered at the grave. Sulphur burned my nose and coated my tongue. I pulled out a handkerchief and held it up to my nose. I noticed that the others, save Holmes, did the same.

The mound was almost identical to the Oakencrest hidey-hole in that it melded in with a hillside. It was impossible to calculate the measurements, but it seemed to be as big as, if not bigger than, Oakencrest's.

Homes stopped at the back side of where the mound melted into the hillside and we followed suit. "I will do reconnaissance. Watson, be on point." He motioned for us to remain as he crept stealthily towards the top of the mound. I watched him and marveled at how fluid his movements were, like a spider crawling up a web towards an unsuspecting prey. Suddenly, Holmes became deathly still and flattened himself against the mound. He waved at us to fall to the ground and we did as commanded. With my face to the ground, I was blind to what was happening, but I could hear the sound of water splashing and a man shouting, "All right! All right! Give me a minnit, cantcha? Can't a man relieve himself in peace?!"

Moments later, I felt a boot nudge my head.

"Watson. Get up." Holmes pointed to the top of the mound. "There's a smoke hole at the top. I was able to get a quick glance before Mr. Potts had to answer the call of nature. Mrs. Dowell, I am happy to report that Mr. Todd is there. Badly beaten, but still alive. And, best of all, there are three men arguing over what to do with young Mr. Todd. Potts, Tyrone and a third man... the young Mr. Colin Leerson, whom I suspect is the leader of this trio."

"Colin?" I couldn't help myself but shake my head in amazement. "The lad back at the hotel?"

"The very same. An enterprising lad, I wager. The windfall

from this silver hoard would be enough to finance quite a future for a young man." He turned towards the Diogenes agents and smiled. "It looks as though both of our needs will be met tonight. You did come armed?" The two men nodded. "Excellent. Watson, have your revolver at the ready. Mrs. Dowell, I have no fear that you have something about you handy?"

Mrs. Dowell did a slight bow of her head and smirked, "My dear Mr. Holmes, a lady always has something at hand." She pulled out a beautiful Oriental fan with a mother of pearl handle.

With the flip of her wrist, it expanded into a mural of a beautiful woman surrounded by a flock of beautifully colored peacocks. She pushed a pearl button on the handle and five sharp, stiletto blades jutted out like silver spines. "And if that is too exotic, I have other more mundane items." She reached under her corset and retrieved a small derringer. "I have other toys on me, if you have the time?"

Holmes barked out a laugh. "Ha! A phenomenal specimen! Then let's be off!"

"Wait," Agent Gordon said, "and what about you?

"Me?"

"Yes, you." The young man lifted his chin and stared down at Sherlock Holmes. "What are you bringing to the fight?"

"Dear boy. I'm bringing this," Holmes said tapping his temple. "It has always been enough in the past. So, follow me but be quiet! We don't want to spook them into action against Mr. Todd. Agent Featherton, leave the saddlebag here. I'm sure it will be safe. We will all need to be able to move freely if the worst happens."

CHAPTER TWELVE

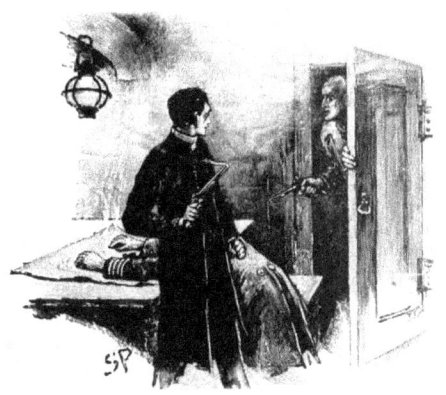

THE SMUGGLER'S MOUND

We stopped at the entrance to the mound. A feeble light from a lantern cut through the early evening gloom and a young man's voice poured out.

"No! No! Not another one. I can't... I won't... this isn't the plan!"

"Yeah, well, you see, *sir*," a seedier, older voice answered him. "Plans change. A sophisticated sort of man understands that, see? And moves with it. Ain't that the truth, Potts?"

"Aye. I never planned on dressing up as a dead girl for one."

"Truth! And gallivanting around the city, looking that fool Holmes and getting my thumb broke. That wasn't in the deal either, wuzzit? So, this poor sap here... well it's just one more hitch, ain't it? One more Gordian knot that needs to get cut, as it were. Do you see my meaning, *sir*?"

"No, no, no," Colin protested. "I never wanted anyone to get hurt! That was your doing... both of you. Not mine... not mine! My plan was simple: melt the silver, sell it and buy back my homestead. No one was supposed to get hurt."

"Well, *sir,*" Sherlock Holmes said as he entered the room. "There are three planted a half mile down the road that would argue otherwise."

"Aye!" Robbie Tyrone cocked his pistol with his free hand and pointed it at Holmes. "And you are destined to be the fourth, you nosey devil!"

Agents Gordon and Featherton stepped in behind Holmes. They held a pistol in each hand. Mrs. Dowell and I followed in behind them, holding our pistols. I spotted Ulysses K. Todd tied and propped up in a corner. He was alive but barely conscious. There was a deep gash on his forehead that needed bandaging and his left eye looked swollen shut. The doctor in me itched to attend to him as soon as possible. I recognized the thugs, that I now knew as Potts and Tyrone, from the train. Tyrone's bandaged hand looked swollen and painful. The fat man Potts wasn't quite so fearsome with his shillelagh while wearing a dress.

In the center of the room was a large black cauldron where Potts would smelt the silver. Alongside it was several cast iron molds, in which to pour the hot liquid and form bricks. The finished product was then stacked into boxes and shipped out to a buyer.

"There are six guns against one," Holmes said. "I think you need to reconsider the odds, Tyrone."

Colin Leerson fell to his knees clasped his hands around his head and began sobbing. "Don't shoot! I'm sorry! So sorry! Please... don't shoot!"

"Sweet Mercy. I always knew you were useless, boy. Stand up like a man!" a deep voice behind me said. I felt cold metal pressed against the back of my neck. "Don't move, Dr. Watson. If any of you move, I'm liken to have a twitch and boom, boom, boom goes the good doctor's head. Might well mess up your pretty dress, Mrs. Dowell. You two up front. Put your guns down on the ground and kick them away. Good lads. Well taught, I can tell. Now, take two steps... good... and turn to face me."

We did as he asked. This choreography turned our party

backwards. Mrs. Dowell and I lead the way, followed by the Diogenes agents and behind them Holmes. In front of me, the landlord, Eric Donnelly, filled the entire doorway with his malevolent presence. Over his shoulder was the saddlebag Agent Featherton had left behind.

"Speaking of plans... this isn't what I had planned either, boy. You see, I knew about the silver. Hell's bells! It's town lore! Everybody knows but nobody properly believed it existed. But I did. It was what brought me here in the first place. I was biding my time. Married your mum, got a proper position in the community, got the lay of the land, searched when I could. Little did I know that the runt of the litter was trying to bite off the prime teat right from under me!"

"How did you find out?" I asked.

"That skinny little twit from the Psychical Society came running into the pub saying he'd been waylaid by robber barons loaded down with silver. Nobody paid him no mind. He eventually took a hansom towards Norfolk, to report it to the proper authorities. Speaking of which, is one of them poor devils buried up yonder one of those 'authorities'? Tsk, tsk. Killing a policeman, boy. I'm seeing a hanging in your future, I am."

"No! It weren't me! It was them. Those two there. Potts and Tyrone. They killed them all by themselves!" The boy started sobbing again. "I didn't have anything... anything to do with the killin's... you have to believe me! I just wanted the silver!"

"I believe you, boy. I know you don't have the water to gut a fish, much less kill a man. But that don't matter. I won't let you hang. That's a saving grace, but I can't let you get away with trying to cheat me either. Any of you."

"You don't truly expect to kill all of us, do you? There are eight against one gunman with a pistol that only holds six bullets," Agent Gordon sneered. "Would you like us to stand in a line to save you the bullets?"

"That won't be necessary, sonny," Donnelly said as he calmly aimed at Gordon's head and pulled the trigger. The sound of the gunshot reverberated inside the mound to match the thunderclaps outside and the agent fell dead. I heard a scream, a crash as someone knocked over a lantern and we were all plunged into the dark. Potts quickly relit the lantern and Donnelly returned his aim to the group.

"You two, next to Colin. I suspect you are in this with him, yes? Want to die with him? No? Pick up those guns and come over here with me. And for God's sake, take off that dress!"

Potts and Tyrone did what they were told, picked up the agent's guns and stood beside their new employer.

"Good lads. You know where your bread is buttered. Now, I think you will see that the tally is a tad bit more in my favor, ain't it?" Donnelly aimed the brushed silver barrel of his pistol straight at my chest. "It is nothing personal, Doctor. I really do love your stories. Pity there will not be any more."

A thick cragged shape swung out of the darkness behind Donnelly, slamming down on his gun, and breaking the bones in his hand. The next to go down were Potts and Tyrone with swift, deadly blows to their heads. As they fell, Holmes stepped into the lighted room swinging the late Pott's shillelagh in a low curve, shattering the landlord's knees and dropping him to the floor. He lay there, screaming in pain as Holmes picked up the gun and pocketed it. "Oh, I don't know. There might be at least one more story to tell, don't you agree, Watson?"

CHAPTER THIRTEEN

A BOTHERSOME COMPANION

Agent Featherton rushed in and shackled the deceptive Mr. Donnelly, not taking very much care as to his injuries. He then took off his jacket and covered Agent Gordon's face. Mrs. Dowell went to him and put her lovely arm over his shoulder as they comforted each other.

Shortly afterwards, the rain clouds outside burst and a horrible storm rolled in. Holmes pulled a latch to cover the smoke hole to keep us dry as we waited for it to pass. He picked up the saddlebag of silver and perched on one of the wooden pallets. Once comfortable, he pulled out a pipe and tobacco from a hidden pocket, God only knew where, and smoked. He was still as a stone as his mind went over the events of the evening, dissecting and sorting through it all.

I kept busy with Mr. Todd. After untying him and doing a thorough field examination, I concluded his injuries to be a minor concussion but not as worrying as I had feared. "A good hot bath, some food and you'll be right as, well, rain!"

Mr. Todd said nothing. He simply stared, open eyed, as if in awe, at Holmes who sat motionless across the room. I worried that Ulysses was in shock. I had seen this sort of look on lads who had just experienced their first battle. His pale blue eyes had a feverish glaze. "Did you hear me, Mr. Todd?" I snapped my fingers by ear to get a reaction. "Mr. Todd!"

"Look at him, Dr. Watson. Sherlock Holmes." He drew the name out, so it sounded strange to my ears. "Sherrrrlock Hollllmes. See how he sits there, so perfectly still?"

I cast an eye towards my friend. I was very familiar with his eccentric mannerisms as old roommates learn to accept. I would leave the flat for hours only to return with him in the exact same position, the only change being the amount of pipe smoke clouding up the air. He was thinking. His brain running like a steam engine on tracks we lesser humans could barely imagine. I suppose it might seem alarming to outsiders but, to me, it was just one of his ways.

"Yes, Mr. Todd. I see him. He is thinking. Probably ruminating over the past few hours, adding up sums of things that went right, things that went wrong. It is his way."

"Ha." Todd shook his head slowly. He whispered, "No one will understand. No one will believe me. Damn them."

He attempted to stand but was having difficulty. I offered assistance but Todd growled and slapped at my hands. "I can do it!"

"You have a concussion, young man! You need to rest and conserve your energy. Please, listen to me, Mr. Todd. I'm a doctor."

Todd got to his feet and steadied himself before turning to me and saying, "Oh, I've had my fill of doctoring, Doctor."

He staggered over to where Holmes sat, and I followed closely behind him. Todd tapped Holmes on the shoulder and whispered something into his ear.

Holmes puffed on his pipe and arched a brow. "Is that so?"

Todd nodded, grimacing at the action. He smiled and pointed a finger at Holmes. "You know it is true. I saw you. No one else did because they were all looking at the door but me... I SAW YOU."

"Ulysses?" Mrs. Dowell said as she pulled herself away from Agent Featherton. "What is wrong?"

"It seems that Mr. Todd here is laboring under the delusion that I am not me." He gripped the pipe even harder between his teeth as he grinned. "I'm a doppelganger. Some Fae charlatan trick."

"He's a changeling! The real Sherlock Holmes is still enslaved at the Fairy Court!"

"Oh, Ulysses..." Mrs. Dowell's eyes welled with tears. "Oh, please... please, don't."

"I saw him! I did, Bernadine. Please, believe me. I saw him transmutate into smoke and transmaterialize through the walls! How do you explain how he made his way outside? How? Do you see any doors, any windows? No! No *human being* could do what he did. It was magic! You all saw it!"

Just then a very wet, irritated police constable followed by a very thin, wiry bespectacled man burst into the room.

"That's the man, right over there, Officer! And those two... down there on the floor... oh my."

"Oi! What's going on here, then?" said the constable. He took one look at the dead men on the floor. "Blimey! What IS going on here?"

Agent Featherton pulled out his identification. "I think I can answer your question, Constable," and pulled the police officer over to one side.

"Oliver!" Todd ran towards the shivering thin man. "My old friend, Oliver, from the Society. You will understand! Remember the odd readings we were receiving on the electrospectrascope transponder? The fluctuations, the energy bursts?"

"Yes, I remember... before those villains crushed it. The needles were bouncing all over the scales. You hypothesized that it was the other side trying to communicate." He pulled his glasses off and tried to dry them with his wet shirt. He gave up and finally just slipped them into his trouser pants. "Something about how much energy they'd need to cross dimensional thresholds or something."

"Yes! They would need tremendous energy to cross the dimensions. For *something* to cross over to our world!" Todd pointed at Holmes.

"Who?" Oliver squinted. "Sherlock Holmes?"

Holmes did a mock bow.

"He's not what he seems. He's a changeling. From the fairy court."

Holmes shrugged his shoulders and smiled brightly.

"*Sherlock Holmes?!*" Oliver pushed Todd away. "Now, that breaks the camel's back that does, Ulysses. You are balmy! Everybody warned me but, no, I tried to be nice because of your bum leg. To think I was going to petition your membership to the Society. I'd be a laughingstock to sponsor you!"

"NO, no, no... Oliver... listen to me... please. It's true! Sherlock Holmes is a fairy changeling! I saw it. Listen to me!" Todd yelled as he staggered after Oliver who, to lose him, rushed outside into the rain.

"Sweet Lord! It never ends." Mrs. Dowell cast a sad look at Agent Featherton, who only nodded and smiled as she dashed after her young, mad ward. "Ulysses K. Todd, wait!"

Holmes laughed and pinched the bridge of his nose. "Oh, that poor Mrs. Dowell. What a bothersome companion to be burdened with, don't you think, Watson?"

"Oh, I think I have some idea of her burden, Holmes."

He rolled his eyes. "I am sure that I have no idea of what you mean."

"So, go on, then, tell me," I said as I sat down with him on the wooden pallet. "How did you do it?"

"Do what? You'll need to elaborate, old sport. I've had some very active days as of late."

"Make your way outside? In a room with only one door leading to and from, without anyone seeing?"

"Magic?"

"Holmes..."

"Are you sure you aren't happy with the idea of magic? Fairy dust suits your readership much better."

"Blast you and your criticism! Just tell me!"

"Fine, as you wish." He pulled ups his legs and sat cross legged as he started his tale. "It's simple, Watson. First of all, Donnelly asking the group to turn around was a marvelous stroke of luck as it put me in the background and out of his view. The damn fool had no idea I was even there. I waited for my chance to strike which came during all the confusion after the shooting of Agent Gordon, I knocked over a lantern giving me a few moments of darkness. I grabbed the shillelagh and a hammer that was lying near the smelting pot, went towards the back and smashed my way through the wall. All of these are made in the same design so I deduced that there would be a similar hidden door where there was on the Oakencrest's mound. I found it, smashed through, went to the front, and saved the day. Simple."

"Yes, that is... simple." I fear the disappointment bled into my voice.

"Don't worry, Watson." Holmes took a deep drag on his pipe and blew out a heavy cloud. "I'm sure you will find a way to make it more dashing when you write it up!"

THE END

ABOUT THE AUTHOR

AGE 6, THE SHAMAN YEARS

Nikki Nelson-Hicks has been described as the "Undisputed Queen of the Warped and the Weird" and the "unholy child of H.P. Lovecraft and Flannery O'Connor."

She finds both terribly amusing.

She has always loved the weird and fantastic. It takes an entire lifetime to get this bizarre.

All of her stories can be found on Amazon in either Kindle or print.

BE CAREFUL WHERE YOU DIG.

There is something very wrong in the Gobi Desert.

"Gruff Springs proves why Nelson-Hicks is the undisputed Queen of the Warped and the Weird." – Paul Bishop, author of 52 Weeks * 52 Western Novels.

Deliliah Ditch, an orphan and woman with no means, becomes a mad scientist's prototype for the Super Soldier that the Angels want him to build.

She has other ideas.

Why do all the women in Poe's life die?

Amy Angler believes she has the answer but needs one more
piece of the puzzle to prove it.

Two con artists bluff the aristocracy
with promises to oust their supernatural squatters.
The tables are turned when it turns out that their foe is quite real
and the con runs much deeper

The entire six story saga of the Accidental Detective series

with extra vignettes and a teaser for the seventh story,

SILVER SCREENS, STACKS OF GOLD AND A BLOODY NOSE

www.ingramcontent.com/pod-product-compliance
Lightning Source LLC
Chambersburg PA
CBHW051921220626
47052CB00003B/537